BONY AND THE
BLACK VIRGIN

Napoleon Bonaparte, the Australian half-caste detective, arrives in the drought-stricken outback of New South Wales, where at Lake Jane, the desolate sheep station belonging to Old Man Downer and his son Eric, two men have been savagely beaten to death. Clues are difficult to unearth in this vast, sandblown country, but Bony's uncanny understanding of the Bush and the people who live there—both black and white—leads him patiently and inexorably towards a solution of this deceptively simple crime. It is a strange solution, and even Bony is horrified at the tragic outcome of his investigations.

D1512777

By the same author in PAN Books

BONY AND THE MOUSE

THE WILL OF THE TRIBE

CAKE IN THE HAT BOX

MURDER MUST WAIT

BONY BUYS A WOMAN

THE BACHELORS OF BROKEN HILL

CONDITIONS OF SALE

This book shall not, by way of trade or otherwise, be
lent, re-sold, hired out or otherwise circulated without
the publisher's prior consent in any form of binding or
cover other than that in which it is published and without a similar condition including this condition being
imposed on the subsequent purchaser

BONY AND THE
BLACK VIRGIN

ARTHUR UPFIELD

UNABRIDGED

PAN BOOKS LTD : LONDON

By arrangement with
WILLIAM HEINEMANN LTD
LONDON

First published 1959 by Wm. Heinemann Ltd.
This edition published 1962 by Pan Books Ltd.,
33 Tothill Street, London, S.W.1

2nd Printing 1967

© by Arthur Upfield 1959
All Rights Reserved

Printed in Great Britain by
Cox & Wyman Ltd., London, Reading and Fakenham

CONTENTS

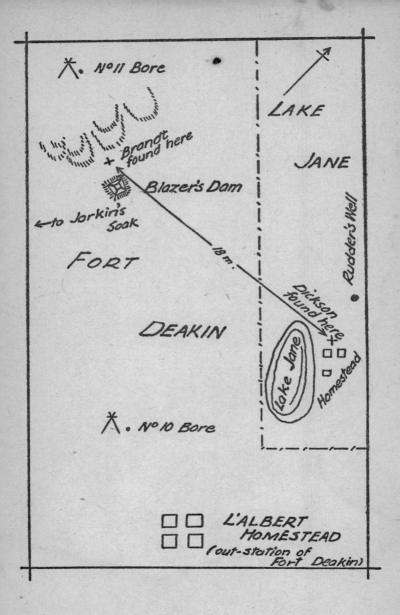

PART ONE

CHAPTER 1

The Downers Go Home

WHAT'S TO be done with a cunning father you have to chase from pub to pub? The truck is serviced and loaded with stores, and everything is ready for the hundred-and-ten miles of blazing track to the old homestead; and the Old Man has to be chased from pub to pub.

In this third year of severe drought covering the western half of New South Wales and a third of Queensland, there were three hotels in Mindee, on the River Darling, each within trotting distance of the others. They were oases within the shadows cast by stately pepper trees, and it was natural for anyone leaving one of them to make a straight line, or as straight as possible, to the next one.

Old Man Downer was a knowledgeable man. He entered a hotel by the front, ranged to the bar counter, ordered a quick 'un, paid, winked at the barman, and departed via the back yard. There he would skulk like a film spy until his son entered the bar to inquire after him, and would trot swiftly to the next hotel. And every barman in cahoots with him.

There stood the Downers' truck outside the only garage, and there angrily stalked young Eric Downer, into and out of the three hotels. And under a vast red gum tree in the small central space of Mindee stood Sergeant Mawby, a bear-like man who moved lazily and spoke softly, and was ever gentle save when preserving the peace.

"You looking for your father?" he inquired mildly of young Eric Downer. "I just saw him go into the River Hotel."

Hot, and furiously angry, Eric halted before the sergeant. He was of average height, supple, nervously alert; his grey eyes were in sharp contrast to the sun-blackened face. A good school had left merely a faint trace of the back-country accent.

"You know how it is, Sergeant."

9

"Yes. Up to his tricks again, eh? Longer he's in town, the more active he gets."

"He knows full well it's time we headed for home. He knows I've the truck loaded and ready to pull out. He's had a good binge—a month of it. He goes on like this every year. Break a feller's heart."

"Got his good points," commented the policeman, a chuckle rumbling low in his throat. "Never any trouble. Always polite and well-behaved. They don't make 'em like him these days, Eric. Anyway, I agree he's had it. You go in the front of the River Hotel, and I'll snaffle him when he comes out by the back."

"You won't charge him?" asked Eric, uneasily. "Have to get going, you know."

"I know my job, young feller." Mawby's eyes were minus guile. "Your dad would be the last character I'd jug."

"Thanks." Eric strode into the River Hotel. "Seen the Old Man?" he asked, glaring at the barman.

"Was here a minute ago. Must be out back," replied the publican, smirking. "Bit hard to locate this morning?"

Eric passed from the bar, along a passage, into the back yard, and from there, via a side lane, to the open space. Then he saw Sergeant Mawby escorting a man one-fifth his size, and half his height, towards the parked truck. The captive was urged up into the driving cabin and the policeman leaned nonchalantly against the imprisoning door. His dark-brown eyes lazily surveyed the captive.

"As I just told your son, Downer, you've had it," he said. "Now you're all set for home. If I see you again in Mindee this side of Christmas, I'll jug you."

"You got no right!" shouted Downer. "I always behave. I'm not a bum or a pest. I'm sober as a judge."

He was better dressed than a judge. He was wearing a new suit, the creases knife-edged. On his white hair sat a new velour hat. The moustache matching his hair was neatly trimmed. He was a dynamo of a man which the whisky of three hotels had failed to slow down.

"Anyhow, so long, Sergeant," he shouted. "Thanks for everything, and to hell with you."

Sergeant Mawby grinned. Downer winked. Sergeant Mawby winked. The truck moved off.

At the edge of town, he shouted to his son:

"Always know when I'm beat, lad. Got everything aboard?"

"Without any help from you," returned Eric, still savage.

"You didn't forget the reviver, did you?"

"Forgot nothing, with no help from you, as I said."

"Someone told me the river's coming down," continued the old man, placatingly.

"To hell with the river."

"That's right! That's right, keep on arguing," yelled Downer. "The booze don't agree with you, that's what. Keep your clapper shut if you don't want to talk, and let me doze a bit. Damn the hat." Snatching off the headgear, he threw it to the floor, and placed his elastic-sided boots hard down on it. After that, in ten seconds, he was asleep.

This Australia does strange things to men. Some men it frightens almost to death, and drives them back to the coastal cities where they can browse like steers in a herd. Other men it cures. With the heat of the sun, and the abrasive action of wind and sand grains, it cures as smoke will cure sides of bacon. Here was old Downer, well over seventy, and one could judge him to be not older than sixty. Here was his son, twenty-six, and looked ten years older. Cured, such men remain impervious to change, physically and mentally.

There was a fence gate ten miles upriver, and at this stop Eric made his father a trifle more comfortable, and smoked a cigarette. For a month they had let go the problems imposed by a seemingly never-ending drought, and each had 'played' in his own manner. Now town had become a bore, and the call of home was strong although the return meant continuing worries.

The road was but a track, iron-hard over the clay-pans and sand-clotted on the red spurs. There was no ground covering, no grass, herbage or shrubs, nothing beneath the red gums bordering the river, nothing within sight which could support a goat. The river was reduced to a stream running sluggishly in a ditch.

Some time later, when they were passing a desolate settler's house, dogs ran out to bark a welcome rather than an alarm, and John Downer heaved himself up from the pit of insobriety.

"Parker's," he said. "Time for a snifter, lad."

"Hold it. We'll boil the billy at the Cliff," decided Eric.

"Can't wait," moaned Downer. "Cliff's nine miles to go."

"That's where we'll have the snifter."

In the stunned condition Downer found himself, he hunted

for pipe and tobacco, and swayed to the rocking of the truck as he tried to slice chips from a plug. Presently he surrendered, saying:

"Give us a cancer stick. Crook when a feller ain't let down to fill his pipe."

Eric extracted a cigarette from a packet in the dashbox, and managed to ignite it. His father fumbled it to his mouth, drew twice, spat out of the window before tossing the cigarette out, too. He said something about fags being good enough for girls and town twirps. The nine miles for him were ninety.

Where the track skirted a river bend, a hundred feet above the dry bed, Eric gave the old man a moderate tot of whisky before brewing a billy of tea. The tea his father wouldn't drink, until threatened that before he did, and ate a slice of bread and cold mutton, he should not have another tot.

"Like your mother, rest her soul," snarled old John. " 'Do this and do that. And *you* go easy on the drink, and don't *you* smoke so much, and you . . .' Oh, hell! . . ."

"And she said to me, 'You look after your father, Eric,'" swiftly added the son. Then, cheerfully, "One thing about you is, you can keep on your feet. Next time I'm ready to leave town, I'll apply to Mawby first, rather than delay, to snaffle you."

"Yes, I suppose you will. The modern generation! Always out to control their parents. Still, you done your job, lad, and your mother would have cheered you on. Rest her soul!"

Fifty miles upriver from Mindee, they reached the main homestead of Fort Deakin, to be welcomed by Midnight Long, the manager, and Mrs Long. They were given the mail for the out-station called L'Albert, and vegetables, as the garden at L'Albert was now a dust heap.

It was forty-eight miles to L'Albert, and another twelve miles to the Downers' homestead at Lake Jane, and once away from the river trees, the plane of the hot October sky pressed upon the plane of the sleeping earth, with no shadows between, and no depth or perspective for man's eyes to register in the steady colourless glare.

John Downer's tongue was arid when they arrived at L'Albert, where they were warmly welcomed by the overseer, Jim Pointer, Mrs Pointer, and their daughter Robin. Mrs Pointer urged them to stay for dinner, but the Downers were anxious to be home.

"Seen anything of Brandt?" asked John of the large Jim Pointer.

"Was over two weeks back," replied Pointer. "Things bad, like everywhere. He complained of isolation at your place, saying it wouldn't be so bad if you'd linked up with a telephone."

"Do that when the drought breaks," grumbled Downer. "Should have done it years back, but you know how it is, with the price of wire and all."

"And the price of whisky," smilingly added the overseer.

"Wouldn't have a snifter to hand, I suppose?" suggested the old man, and was given a head shake and a reminder of Midnight Long's attitude towards drink on his station.

Knowing that Carl Brandt, who had been left in charge at Lake Jane, was a poor cook, Mrs Pointer gave them a batch of bread, and some of the vegetables brought from the main homestead. She was short and rotund, and inclined to giggle, and often almost eager to give the entire contents of her house. Following a short conversation with vivacious Robin Pointer, Eric slid in behind the wheel, and started on the final stage to Lake Jane.

"You doing any good with Robin?" asked John, with feigned casualness.

"Same as usual," the son answered. "You interested?"

"Course I'm interested. You're getting on. Time you was married. And besides, it's time there was another woman at Lake Jane. You're taking over pretty sound like, relieving me of the running of the place. I don't find anything wrong with Robin."

"Then you marry her."

"Me! Talk sense." John skidded away from the subject. "Hope Carl Brandt been looking after the sheep properly. Looks like there's been plenty of wind lately. Road's clean of even truck tracks."

They came to the boundary of their property where on a sheet of tin wired to the gate was the announcement, 'Lake Jane . . . Five Miles'.

Lake Jane! A lake! A lake in this paralysed, waterless waste! Lake Jane was a depression, egg-shaped, three miles wide, pocked with brittle herbal rubbish which would powder if trodden upon, dark and repellent. The narrow beach was cement hard, white against the encircling sand dunes, and offering a racing track. On the far side of the 'lake' the Downers' homestead gleamed under the sun.

As they followed the curving beach, the distant homestead moved gradually towards their front, and presently the old man said:

·"Something wrong with the mill; looks like it's broke."

"Could be," snapped Eric. "Can't trust anyone these days to look after the place."

The beach ended at a bar of coarse grey sand, named the Crossing, over which past floods had poured into Lake Jane. Eric revved the engine when on the sand, dropped into low gear, and pressed hard on the accelerator, keeping the loaded vehicle on the move. Three hundred yards of this, and when they roared up the incline towards the homestead the radiator was boiling.

The homestead gate was closed, and when John got down to open it Eric sat crouched forward over the steering wheel. The mill just beyond the house was stationary and two of its vanes hung brokenly from the head. No smoke rose from the house chimney. Between the gate and house grew a box tree. In the shade was a dog's kennel. A Queensland heeler appeared from the kennel and opened his jaws to bark a greeting. No sound resulted.

A soft wind came from the house, and this wind brought a message.·

CHAPTER 2

The Dead

DUE TO a long career when rapid decisions had to be made, the metamorphosis of John Downer on returning to the truck was not remarkable. Here was crisis, and evidence of devotion to John Barleycorn was erased. The words came sharply.

"The stink of death is about the place, lad. Let's prospect."

Crisis now appeared to lie heavily on the younger man, and, without speaking, he nodded and backed down from the truck, to gaze stonily at the dog collapsed outside its kennel, and beyond it to the frightened house.

"Dog's all in," commented John. "Been there for days."

A sob of profound commiseration broke from Eric, and he would have stopped had not his father said:

"Not now, lad. Must see what's happened to Brandt. Come on."

The house faced the wasteland of the lake. It was built of pine logs under an iron roof. It was commodious and along its front was a ten-feet-wide veranda reached by a flight of steps. The living-room was large and fairly well furnished – the kitchen range and wash-bench at one end, and beside the range the doorway leading to the wide space at the rear. There was evidence of a struggle, the dining table being slanted away from normal, the brass oil lamp lying on the floor, chairs overturned. Bric-à-brac massed on a side table, objects of utility on the mantel over the stove, crocks on the dresser – all were covered with a film of red dust.

The two bedrooms were undisturbed. The small off-room, used as an office, bore no sign of disturbance. In through the open back door came persistently the smell of death.

"Been a fight, looks like," remarked John Downer. "Days back, too; like with the heeler, poor bastard. Brandt must be dead in his room, by the stink." Looking intently at Eric, he noted the pallor greying the suntan, and added: "You stay here, lad. I'll prospect out back."

Eric, however, followed his father. As they stepped from the rear door to the sanded ground beside the almost empty house rain-tank, the scene confronting them comprised the well and its raised coping with the mill astride over it, the reservoir tank and the short drinking-trough. Beyond the well was the long, open-faced machinery shed and workshop, flanked on the left by the hired hand's room, and on the right by the harness room and store.

"Mill damaged by the wind 'cos it wasn't braked," John said, but his eyes were directed to the ground swept clean of prints by the wind. Away to the left was the fowl house and netted yard, and near-by, under another box tree, two kennels with no dogs in evidence.

They proceeded to the room provided for the hired hand, when he was employed, which was supposed to be occupied now by Carl Brandt. It was empty. The mattress on the bed was denuded of Brandt's blankets. The bedside table bore nothing but dust. The clothes-pegs were naked. On the floor was scattered a pack of cards.

15

They found the body on the earth floor of the machinery shed and close to the rear wall. It was lying on its back, with one arm thrust outward, and the other by the side, one leg drawn up. Their own tracks to it were the only marks on the wind-levelled ground.

"It's not Carl Brandt," whispered Eric, his breath coming quickly.

"Stranger to me, lad. Don't get it. Been dead for days, by the look of him. What's that in his fist?"

"Don't know. Looks to be . . . It's a lock of someone's hair."

"So it is. Could be he grasped it as he died, tore it from his killer's head. Yes, could be. And that wouldn't be Carl Brandt. Now where the hell is Brandt?"

Both were now anxious to be out of the shed, and, outside, they gazed about as men wholly undecided what next to do; until Eric proceeded to the dog kennels near the fowl house.

The chains attached to them entered the dark interior. Eric fell to his knees to gaze into a kennel, then reached inside and withdrew the body of a half-grown kelpie. He withdrew from the second kennel another kelpie, also dead, and, standing again, knelt down at them, mute and frozen with horror.

It was not yet finished. Within the netted yard were the twenty-odd fowls, all dead of thirst.

The sun was low in the west, and the little wind had died. It was completely silent, as, the water trough being empty, there were no crows present.

"I don't get it," admitted old John, his lips trembling.

"I do," Eric said, and there was hate in his eyes. "Carl Brandt killed that stranger, and then he cleared out and left the dogs chained up and the fowls without water. The dirty swine. The heeler . . ."

He left, running to skirt the house to reach the blue heeler, tougher than the kelpies, and still alive. The old man trudged away to the shearing-shed, hoping to find tracks, and found nothing left by the wind to read. Weather-wise, he was convinced that the tragedy had occurred not less than a week previously. In that period the wind had often been wild and hot with early spring.

Now that he was familiar with the problem, the tension subsided in John Downer's mind, and the physical stresses imposed by age and a month's hard drinking returned. He found Eric at the back door. The heeler had been placed on

16

the ground beneath the rain-tank, and Eric was permitting the tap to drip water on the animal's saliva and sand-caked grinning jaws. The dog's eyes were partially open, and they, too, were caked with dust.

"Me and that dog's alike, lad. We both need a snort," rasped John. "Fetch the bottle."

Eric left for the truck, and John knelt beside the heeler and carefully raised its head. There was no recognition, no response, and gently he laid it down and fought to master the trembling in his hands, which flowed upward through his arms and down to reach his heart. He accepted the whisky bottle from Eric and called for a pannikin.

The long swig of neat spirit coursed through him and banished the tremors. He half filled the pannikin with water and added whisky, opened the dog's jaw and dripped the diluted spirit into its mouth. At first it dribbled out, and then the body shuddered and the throat muscles worked to permit swallowing. Breathing came with the sound of a man sawing wood.

"Might save him," said John, standing. "Here, take a nip, lad. Then we'll get to hell out of here, boil the billy, and think what we have to do. Back to the truck. You bring the heeler."

They drove half a mile to the junction of a track with that to L'Albert, where John made a fire and Eric filled the billy, and this common chore helped them both back to normality, the father ready to become subordinate to the son he had encouraged to lead.

"What d'you reckon?" he asked.

"We'll have to go back to L'Albert and the telephone," Eric replied. "Have to contact Mawby and report all this."

"Yes, I suppose we ought, lad. What about the sheep, though? Have to see to them. Rudder's Well might be broken down or something."

"The sheep'll have to wait. We have a murder on our hands, remember."

John Downer felt disappointment as he watched his son toss half a handful of tea into the boiling water and lift the billy off the fire with a stick. Abruptly explosive, he shouted:

"Sheep wait, be damned! They're all we got left of nine thousand. Lose them, and we walk off Lake Jane."

"Our job is to report to the police as soon as possible. You know that," argued the now stubborn Eric.

"To hell and gone with the police!" John continued to shout. "Our job's to look out for the sheep. The feller in the shed ain't dying for lack of water, and Brandt'll be lying snug by this time. Damn him, damn him to hell! What a mess to come home to."

Eric said, sipping hot tea and nibbling a biscuit:

"All right, then. We go out to Rudder's. We unload at the shed there. You camp there for the night, and I'll run back to Jim Pointer's place and use their telephone. That suit?"

"Yes. Should of worked it out in the first place. You can plan things when you want."

The heeler lying on the seat between them, they started on the four mile journey to the paddock where existed the remnants of the sheep flocks they had built to nine thousand by the beginning of the drought. The entire stock watered at the well sunk by a contractor named Rudder.

The sun was gone, and the early evening light tended to magnify the passing scrub trees and the widely scattered bush, whilst the areas of bare sand were salmon-pink, or rippled like purple velvet.

"Can't help wonderin' who that dead feller is," remarked John, determinedly puffing at a sick pipe. "Beats me. Must have come here by the back way, across country from a northern station, perhaps Mount Brown. Has a game of cards with Brandt. One of 'em cheats. There's an argument. That stranger did look bashed to the side of the head, didn't he?"

"Don't let's talk about it, Dad," pleaded Eric. "What a day! What a heck of a day!"

"Can't help talking about it, lad. Got to think of Carl Brandt, escaped murderer. He might be holding up out here at Rudder's. Could be anywhere. We've a rifle on the truck, haven't we?"

"The forty-four is under the seat. How's Blue?"

"Got a hope. One eye open, anyway. And there's a wriggle to his tail now you say his name."

They were passing through a belt of spindly mulga when the old man cried cheerfully:

"The mill's still working, lad."

Three minutes later they came to the Rudder's Well paddock, and John alighted to open the gate, and leave it open for Eric to shut on his return. From the gate it was less than half a mile to the well and its windmill, with the canegrass, open-fronted shed a couple of hundred yards their side of it.

"Any sign of Brandt?" asked Eric, concentrating on his driving.

"No, none. No smoke from the fireplace. Couple of crows perched on the roof. The sheep are in to water. Things seem to be all right."

The waning light was steel, the vista of open plain was grey. Above the plain hung a grey dust-fog raised by the sheep, now drinking at the trough line, or, having drunk, lying down a little distance from it.

The truck was stopped at the shed, and Eric volunteered to remove the load while his father took the rifle and went to the well to see by the marker that the reservoir tank was a third full. It was now too late to look over the sheep, or approach the few cows and a bull which once had been the pride of his heart.

Eric stowed the load within the shed, and set the tucker box and bread and vegetables on the rough table. It was ground-dark when John returned, and the crows were drawn into the silence of night, which seemed to hold apart from the world the plaintive baa-ings of the distant sheep.

"Don't look to be that Brandt's about," John said. "We going to eat before you go?"

"Not me. I'll wait to eat at L'Albert. Your swag's here, and the tucker. The heeler's on a bag by the petrol drums. He's coming good. Could be all right by morning. Now I'd better get on back to the telephone and Mawby."

"Of course, lad. Don't worry about me and the dog. Camp with the Pointers if they ask you to. I left the gate open. You close it. Good luck!"

He watched the departing truck's lights stop at the gateway, saw the vehicle go on into the night of trees beneath the dancing stars. Then, in the shed again, he put a match to a hurricane lamp, and stood eating slices of bread, and fish from a tin, and completed 'dinner' with a dose from the bottle.

Ah, to hell with town! It was good while it lasted but it couldn't beat home and the sheep. He felt it strange, sitting on a case and smoking, that for the first time for what seemed many moons he was able to think, and to survey all the old problems of the drought that came crowding back for attention, plus the new problem of a dead man in his machinery shed, and the hired hand gone on a long journey. Well, to see to the dog, and then for a real long sleep.

The heeler's eyes were wide open to greet him in the lamp-light. The tail wagged, although with effort. The nose was wet and cool, but the head was too heavy to lift.

John opened a jar of meat extract and made a strong broth with cold water. He had to support the dog so that it could drink, and in him was vast pity, for on two memorable occasions he himself had come nigh to death from thirst.

Afterwards he blew out the lamp, and, taking his swag of blankets to a distant bull oak, unrolled them to fashion a mattress. Then he went back for the dog, and eventually he fell asleep with an arm about the heeler, and in his other hand the rifle.

CHAPTER 3

Sergeant Mawby Takes Command

MAN AND dog slept undisturbed, and at break of day John Downer built a fire on the open fireplace in front of the shed, and went back to the tree for the dog and his bedding.

The emaciated animal lay on a bag in the warmth of the fire, which halted for a while the strengthening light of the new day. The old man sipped tea and smoked his pipe while standing and facing outward over the desolate scene to-be. The crows were already cawing.

John Downer was the leaseholder of a hundred and fifty thousand acres of land; a pastoralist, a man of substance – what was left of substance after three years of drought. Sixty years in the past he had entered the ring of life as horse tailer in a droving outfit, and now he was still ahead on points, although the growing daylight would reveal the latest reverses.

Away back in 1930 he had been the Fort Deakin overseer, living at L'Albert with his wife and young Eric. In that year he had been successful with the Western Lands Board in gaining the grant of this hundred and fifty thousand acres resumed from the leasehold of Fort Deakin, which his wife had named Lake Jane because then the lake was full of water. He had built the homestead, made and lost money, had been able to send Eric to a public school in Melbourne.

20

Eric had done so well, too. He had just gained entry to the University to study for a medical degree when his mother died, and in spite of opposition, he had returned home.

John Downer, king of all he could survey, and more, a kingdom of barely less than two hundred and fifty square miles, yet a mere back paddock compared with the great Fort Deakin, which still boasted three-quarters of a million acres. Not quite five feet five inches in his high-heeled boots, his body still hard and rounded, he didn't need glasses to survey his kingdom, and not yet had he to be fitted with dentures. People thought he was nearing sixty, but he knew he was seventy-four.

The casualties! A mulga splinter and tetanus had taken his wife five years before this day, and Nature's withholding of rain had reduced his sheep to a little below a thousand when he and Eric had gone to town for the Annual Bender.

A Kingdom! It needs a stout heart to be king of such.

He had given the dog a mash of meat extract and tinned meat, and had breakfasted on tinned meat and bread, with further pannikins of tea, when Midnight Long arrived in his utility. Long was sparse and tough, fifty and grey. The sobriquet had been bestowed for his habit of returning to his river homestead from an inspection of his run and the sheep long after midnight.

"They want you in at Lake Jane, John," he said, cutting chips for his pipe, and waiting for the old man to load his dog and himself on to the seat beside him. "Eric's busy with Mawby. Things looks pretty bad out here, eh?"

"Could be worse, I suppose," offered John, settling into the utility. "Could be seven hundred sheep left today. Oughtn't to have gone to Mindee on the Annual this year."

"Would have made no difference had you stayed around ... as far as the sheep's concerned. You could have done nothing more than Brandt did while he worked here. I assume he did his job. Always found him dependable."

"Seems to have done it to the time he mur ... the time of the murder."

"Bad show, John. Don't make head or tail of it. I took a look-see at the dead man, and I've never seen him alive. Eric says neither you nor he has, and both Mawby and Constable Sefton have never seen him in Mindee. Now what did Brandt ... But we'll save it. The police will be asking the questions. You know about the river flooding down?"

"Heard in Mindee."

"Biggest river since '27, so they say. Could bring water down the Backwash and fill your Lake Jane."

"So!" mocked Downer. "Reminds me of the mariners' saying: 'Water, water everywhere. And not a blade of grass to eat.' We don't want water trickling over the ground; we want it falling from the blasted sky in floods."

"It'll come from that way, too, as you rightly know. Must come."

"It's a point," agreed the old man, stroking the head of the heeler resting on a thigh. "You all get here this morning?"

"Yes. Mawby and Sefton came to my place late last night, bringing a tracker. The doctor and a police photographer flew out from the Hill this morning. I brought a couple of abos from L'Albert. Looks as though you'll save the heeler. Pity about the kelpies. Not like Brandt to leave 'em all tied up like that. Must have thought they'd follow him, and give him away some place."

Midnight Long braked the utility to a halt before the front steps, and Eric came down from the veranda to meet them.

"Mawby says we may have our own house back," he said, faintly bitter. "He and Sefton are about with the others, and the L'Albert aborigines are burying the dead man away back from the shearing shed. I objected to having him planted in our cemetery, and when I told Mawby to take the body back to Mindee, he didn't seem to like it."

"Couldn't expect him to," remarked Midnight Long dryly.

"Perhaps not," agreed Eric. "Anyway, come on up. Bit early for lunch, but I have a meal ready."

Soon after they reached the living-room, Mawby and his colleagues came in by the rear door. Besides the sergeant, there was a young-looking man, obviously the doctor because he didn't look like a policeman and carried a brown bag; a man who did look like one and who carried a camera; and Constable Sefton, tall, large and mulga-like in outward toughness. The introductions having been made, and hosts and guests seated, Sergeant Mawby took command.

"Nice being here," he said, his brown eyes beaming at the Downers. "Pity about this murder, though. Sort of spoils the day. Ah! Cup of tea! I'll be asking for half a dozen."

"The feller was killed, then?" asked John.

"Doctor Truscott, here, says he was hit with a blunt instrument, as the saying goes; both heavy and blunt. About twenty hits. And no one seems to know who he is. You never saw him before?"

"Not to my knowledge," replied John.

"Must have drifted down from the north. We don't know him in Mindee. What time did you get home yesterday?"

"I told you that," interposed Eric, and blandly Sergeant Mawby pointed out that he was putting the question to his father.

"About five-ish, I think," answered Downer patiently. "Bit hazy about the time. I was sufferin', as you'll understand."

"Don't we all!" agreed Mawby, smiling broadly. "Anyway, it isn't important. What we would like to nail, though, is the time that that feller was killed. Doctor Truscott thinks it was about a week. Nothing alive about the place, except the crows?"

"Only the heeler. We saved him."

"Oh! There was a live dog, then? Chained to his kennel like the others?"

"That's so. He was all in. Must have been there a week."

"Ah! Now that's what I call co-operation. Could you be a little more definite, doctor?"

"An autopsy would have assisted us. . . ."

"Now, doctor, you would not have wanted that feller on the plane with you, and I didn't want him with me all the way to Mindee." Mawby lit his pipe. "Well, Constable Cliff has his pictures. You can sign the death certificate, and Mr Long, being a Justice, can sign for the burial. Before we leave, I'll get you Downers to make a statement of what you found here, and we'll have the abos put their prints to a joint statement of their work this morning."

"There will be an inquest?" murmured Midnight Long.

"Of course, sir. Now there is a little matter I'd like to mention." The sergeant produced a spill of paper, and, pushing back the tablecloth, carefully unrolled the paper to disclose a lock of hair. "This hair was found clutched in the dead man's hand, and it would appear to have been pulled from the head of his killer. According to Doctor Truscott, the first blow to his head mightn't have caused instant death, so we may assume from the hair that there was a struggle, and the disarray in this room indicates that the struggle took place here. Constable Sefton, describe Carl Brandt."

"Age about forty-five. Weight about a hundred and forty. Fair hair tinged with grey at the temples. Blue eyes. Long face. Has a slightly foreign accent."

"So you see, gentlemen, this hair didn't come from the head of Carl Brandt."

John Downer, sitting next to the sergeant, leaned sideways to look more closely at the lock of hair.

"That hair wasn't pulled from anyone's head," he said sharply. "It's been cut off, either with a sharp knife or scissors."

"Just so, John, just so," agreed Sergeant Mawby.

CHAPTER 4

Some Wells are Deep

JOHN DOWNER took over the chore of preparing lunch, and with him in the kitchen-living-room was Midnight Long, the others being busy outside somewhere, and, according to Eric, rushing around in circles. Downer thoughtfully asked:

"What d'you make of that hair, Mr Long?"

"What do you?" countered the manager.

"Well, it wasn't shorn off Carl Brandt, and it didn't come off the head of the dead stranger. He was a redhead. It didn't come from you, and I'm certain sure it didn't come from Robin Pointer. Could have come from me, but I didn't see any white in it. What I mean is that it could have been cut from me about twenty years ago."

"Then all that's left are the aborigines," deduced Midnight Long.

"Just so. But how do they come into this murder that Brandt must have done? Mawby is saying nothing, but he's thinking hard about that hair. I'm leaving the abos out of it. The funny thing is that it was cut off, not pulled off. I'll tell you something. It was about the time me and Jane took over this country that she got the idea of cutting a lock of hair off young Eric. She sort of mounted it on a card, and then she snipped a lock from me, and mounted it on another card. I can see her now, her eyes bright, and holding the cards one

24

in each hand; Eric's light brown and mine jet black, and after she died I remember going through what she called her Treasure Chest, and seeing them cards of hair in it. I've kept that Chest for all these years, and an hour ago I looked for the cards, and they're not there."

The grey eyes of Midnight Long were shrouded with introspection.

"Does your memory of the hair on the card tally with the lock Mawby's got?"

"Pretty near."

"Then you should tell him about it."

"Suppose I should. All right, I will."

"Anything else missing from the Treasure Chest?"

"Yes. A gold watch with a locket at the back. Picture in it of me when we were married, and a picture of baby Eric we had put in when he was about four months."

"Well, John, you'll have to relate all that to Mawby. Better have him in here at once. By the way, I think there's a few fresh onions on the ute you could slice into that curry. I'll get 'em."

When Sergeant Mawby stepped into the house, John was seated at the table, smoking his pipe, and the preparation for the curry forgotten.

"Mr Long says you want to tell me something, John," the policeman said, sitting also at the table. He listened without comment until the story was done. "Let's have a look at that Treasure Chest. D'you mind?"

"No. But I don't want my Jane's things pulled about. They're sort of sacred, if you know what I mean."

"That'll be jake, John," agreed Mawby.

He was conducted to the main bedroom, and from beneath the old-fashioned double bed John drew a Chinese cedarwood box, exquisitely carved and perfectly kept. He shifted it to the bedspread, which was dulled by dust.

"Nice box," observed Mawby. "You cleaned it recently, I see."

"Yes, dusted it about an hour ago when I came here to look for the hair cards. Always done that every Sunday, you know. I keep a special camel-hair brush, and sometimes I give it a drop or two of oil."

Inwardly Mawby groaned, and another part of him rejoiced. He might not now have to requisition the box for fingerprints.

John lifted the lid, and perfume rose to meet them, strong and sweet.

"I put some scent in now and then," explained John. "The sort my wife always liked. There's her bits and pieces." He unwrapped tissue paper. "Gold bangles and brooches and other bits of jewellery. A wristlet watch she give me, and the rest."

"You sure only her own watch and the locks of hair are missing?" pressed Mawby.

"Yes, I been through it all."

Mawby frowned as the chest was closed and replaced under the bed. A very human man, he was saddened. They heard steps in the outer room, and John thought it was Midnight Long returning with the onions. It was Eric who appeared in the bedroom doorway.

"Did I hear you say you had lost something?" he asked his father, his face concerned.

"Yes, your mother's watch, and two hanks of hair, yours and mine," replied John, and Mawby added:

"Could add up."

"How?" came sharply from the young man.

"Feller came here when Brandt was away looking to the sheep," lugubriously replied the sergeant. "Brandt seen his tracks, crept into the house, found the stranger going through your mother's Treasure Chest, fought him in the kitchen, chased him to the machinery shed, hit him with a blunt instrument. Feller dies with a lock of hair in his fist. Brandt panics. Packs up and clears out. Forgets to replace the watch, but not to put the chest back under the bed. Has the watch in his pocket, or he could have put it somewhere where it'll be found eventually. All tells of panic after killing a man."

"What did he do with the dead man's blanket roll?" pressed Eric. "Feller wouldn't travel without a swag. I've been down the well. The swag wasn't dumped there. I've been through the entire homestead, and can't locate that swag."

"Took it with him to plant somewhere on his way out, could be," replied Mawby. "No time to burn it here. Objective? To destroy identification, or delay it. But we'll identify that body, never fear. Photographs, fingerprints, because the hands are still dry, even the upper denture he had we've collected. Anyway, the robbery could have been the motive for the fight and resultant death. Good enough until we overhaul Brandt."

"Ah! Just thought of it, Sergeant. There's one place where that missing swag could be. In the reservoir tank above the well. I'll look."

Mawby mentioned the cards to which the locks of hair had been sewn.

"Could of been stuffed into the stove," John said. "They weren't back in the Chest, and they weren't anywhere on the floor. Eric lit the fire, remember. Wouldn't think to pull out paper and stuff that might have been in the stove."

"Course not," agreed Mawby. "Well, we'll know more when we collar Brandt. Meanwhile, John, look around and let me have news of anything you find, such as that watch and the missing hank of hair and the cards, and the feller's swag. We're pretty well finished here, for the time being, that is. Have to get busy tracking forward to Brandt, and tracking back to identify the dead man and where he came from."

Shortly after midday John Downer called his guests for lunch, and, having served them, he took a dish of hot curry and rice and slabs of bread and jam to the three aborigines. At one o'clock Mawby departed with Sefton and his tracker, and the doctor with the photographer joined Midnight Long on the seat of the utility, while the two L'Albert station aborigines climbed into the tray-body.

"Hope Mawby keeps his bus moving on the Crossing," John said, standing beside Midnight Long's truck.

"Shouldn't bother him, John. He's strong enough to lift the car over the Crossing, and Sefton's with him. We'll wait and see."

The doctor wanted to lay five shillings that Mawby would bog, and everyone watched the sergeant's car passing down the track and raising a cloud of red dust. The station aborigines, standing at the back, were equally interested, and Eric Downer watched from the rear of the vehicle – watched, not the departing car, but the aborigines.

On one turning about to see if he, too, was wagering silent odds, Eric stepped to the side of the tray-body opposite his father, and, stooping swiftly, drew a figure on the sandy ground.

Looking up, he saw that the aborigine was looking down and witnessed in the dark eyes understanding and the nod of the head. Then, with the edge of a palm, he erased the sand figure.

27

The police car gained the far side of the Crossing, and took to the hard lake beach with accelerating speed, and Midnight Long and his companions bade farewell to the Downers and set off after it. From the veranda, father and son watched the departing vehicles following the circular edge of Lake Jane.

"Well, lad, that's that," drawled old Downer. "A murder and a police investigation. You never know what's waiting round the next bend."

"You're right there. You never know." Eric hesitated before saying: "I'm worn out by the excitement. Any grog left in the bottle?"

"Too right, lad. We'll share it. Then we'll wash up, and by then I'll be ready for a nap."

"And I'll run out to Rudder's for the load."

"And skin those sheep I killed this morning. Thirteen there was. The rest are too far gone." Again in the meal-disordered kitchen, he asked: "Where did you say they'd buried that feller?"

" 'Way back from the shearing shed. Why?"

"Been wondering. I'm glad you told 'em not to bury him in our plot. Still, we'll have to put a rail round him, be decent to the dead. I'll see to it."

Eric stoked the range. He said:

"I'll get going for Rudder's. You clean up."

Eric found him asleep in an easy chair on the veranda, a handkerchief over his face to defeat the flies.

"Never heard you, lad. How did you get on?"

"All right. Took off the skins, and brought the lot home. Did you get any idea how many were left?"

"No. We got there too late last night, and they left too early for me to tally them."

"Brandt seems to have done his job to the time he bolted," Eric said. "We could have eight hundred left living. It's the walking to the water and out to feed that's killing them. Have to think about making camp where there's a bit of feed left, and carting water to them. Ah, the mulga wire's at work."

Beyond Lake Jane, beyond the far horizon of sand dune and patch scrub, was rising a disjointed column of dark smoke, lifting as though to support the westering sun.

"The murder broadcast," agreed John. "Them abos don't need radios and telephones and things."

"No, but we do. A telephone at least is what we must have."

"Suppose we shall, if we're to have any more murders," temporized John, as both watched the rising smoke signal telling of the murder that had happened.

CHAPTER 5

Facets of a Diamond

TO EVERY man his own problems to stir him to effort. Sergeant Mawby and his assistant, Constable Sefton, had their official problem to deal with in addition to any private ones, and, taken together, the Downers had their problem of surviving the drought. The policemen were one when tackling their problem of finding Carl Brandt, but unfortunately the Downers were not united in their approach to the problem of survival.

The long rainless period had so reduced the areas of grazing, relative to the dwindling water supplies, that the last of the Downers' sheep had to be based on Rudder's Well. Already the grazing had been cleaned out for upward of three miles from the water, compelling the sheep to walk that distance there and back to feed.

Thus before the Downers went off to Mindee on their Annual Bender normal routine had been changed. Every morning Eric ran out to the well in the truck, as there wasn't a horse fit to ride, and he would find several of the weakest sheep unable to stand after filling with water and so become the victims of the vicious foxes and the devilish crows. These casualties he would kill in mercy and skin for the wool.

It had been Carl Brandt's chore to go to Rudder's Well every morning, riding his bike, to follow this same routine. Now Eric was returned to it. And every morning he killed half a dozen lingering victims, and every morning therefore the Downers' flock was further reduced. Meanwhile John did the cooking and the house chores, and pottered about the homestead.

On the third morning following the return home, Eric drove at speed less than normal, sitting forward over the steering wheel to maintain careful scrutiny of the winding track just in front of the radiator. This track bore only the marks of his truck . . . until he saw the trail of a snake crossing it.

He was driving so slowly that he was able to stop the truck when athwart that cross track, and, switching off the ignition, he stepped to the ground and listened, hearing nothing but the noise of the wind, a low hissing noise as it passed through the compact branches of the belt of tea tree at this place.

He followed the snake's trail into the tea tree, a shrub-like bush, here eight or nine feet high, small of leaf and untouched by the drought. The snake's trail led in among the tea tree, the ground being clear of vegetation and having a thin coating of salmon-pink sand.

For an hour he was hidden among the tea tree, and when he emerged he was trailing behind him a branch of this robust bush, and thus swept clean his own tracks, and the track of the snake. In his free hand he carried a paper bag.

He used the branch to erase the footprints to the very edge of the track when standing on the truck step, and, tossing the branch into the cabin, manoeuvred himself behind the steering-wheel, and drove on towards Rudder's Well.

His next step was beside a wide clear space about two magnificent sandalwood trees.

Taking the branch and the paper bag with him he walked to the centre of the clear space, where he gathered a few completely dry sticks and twigs, and of them made a fire. Then, with care, he dropped from the paper bag a quantity of long black hair.

The hair smoked but lightly. When it was consumed, he burned the paper bag, and stood awhile until the fire died down, when he scraped a hole with the heel of his boot, enlarged it with his hands, and finally with a twig teased all the fire embers into it, and covered the mass with sand.

Sweeping the fire-site with the branch, he used this again on retreating to the truck, and there tossed the branch aside, and drove on to the well.

2

This morning he had eight sheep to kill and skin, and rack the skins to dry in the sun. From a gay young sheepman he was becoming a mere butcher, taciturn and introspective. The problem facing both him and his father was not being tackled with unity of direction, owing to lack of experience in himself and half a century of wisdom gathered by the old man. At rock bottom Eric Downer was too imaginative, too idealistic, too sensitive, to play the role of a pastoralist when the wolf of adversity had him by the throat.

He had never found hard work an enemy. Erecting a fence or building a shed or repairing a mill or pump were tasks for eager hands to do, things to create. But now, when financial resources were strained and improvement work was out of the question, there was left only the normal working chores, such as going out for a load of firewood.

Homing with such a load, he saw a strange utility near the empty hen yard and Robin Pointer emerge from the house to meet him.

Robin Pointer was good to look at and merited any man's approving smile. She was of medium height and small-boned, and there ended any hint of fragility. She could ride with the best, with or without a saddle, and her narrow long-fingered hands, which could hold a palette and paint brush, and paint rather well, could also check a bad-tempered horse. Today she was wearing a flecked tweed skirt and a lime-green overblouse. Her jet black hair was hatless.

Eric stepped from the truck to greet her. From his higher level he looked down into large dark eyes flecked with gold, and the windows of a mind he had never fathomed.

The contours of her oval face were soft, save about the small chin.

"What brought you?" he asked, as their eyes held in meeting, and even now he found himself trying to read her mind.

"You. I came to see you," she replied. "And at the same time I brought a crate of chooks for you to restock with, and a mutual friend, Constable Sefton."

He was unable to prevent the flash of surprise in his eyes, although his voice was controlled, and he made no attempt to be casual.

"What did he come for? Where is he?"

"Inside, talking with your father. The utility is his, and the chooks are on the back. I'll help you with the crate. And I want to talk to you."

"Why not? I'm easy."

They transferred the birds to the hen yard, admired the

Orpington rooster, and returned the crate to the utility. He brought water from the well to fill the drinking trough, for the fowls would have to remain in the yard for a few days, rinsed his hands, dried them on an oily handkerchief, and said earnestly:

"That was very nice of you, and of your mum and dad, to think of us. How come Sefton brought you?"

"Oh, he arrived this morning, and I just made use of him." The girl regarded Eric seriously, noted the old but serviceable clothes, the cut on a forearm caused by a jagged log end, and also the clean-shaven face and the well-tended hair.

"Sef came to get measurements, so he said. They've found out who the dead man was."

"Who?"

"Name's Dickson. Paul Dickson, plus a few aliases. He was arrested at Hungerford for sheep-stealing, and he broke out of jail a week before you found him in your shed."

"What about Brandt?" Eric asked.

"Seems they haven't caught up with him yet. Sef says it might take time, but they surely will. Make me a cigarette, please."

Eric produced a tin of tobacco and papers and thoughtfully rolled a cigarette and licked the paper for her before tamping the end with a match. Having struck a match, he teased:

"You're becoming pally with Constable Sefton."

"Pally! Don't be silly. Oh, you mean by calling him Sef. Caught that from Dad. Nice enough man." Her eyes grew large as they examined his, seeking the mind behind them. She said:

"Where did you bury that Paul Dickson?"

"Back of the shearing shed. Why?"

"Show me."

"Show you where they buried him?" he echoed. She nodded, and he shrugged and obeyed.

From inside the rear doorway old John watched them, and wondered, hopefully. From a corner of the machinery shed Constable Sefton smiled, winking at himself, believing that he knew much about both. They continued to the shearing shed, passed by it, disappeared. And when they were out of sight, Robin halted, causing Eric to confront her.

"This will do. Kiss me, hard. Hold me in your arms and kiss me."

32

Eric hesitated. Waiting, her face registered passivity, but in her eyes were expectancy and what might be calculation. Of the two, she was now the stronger, and with the fleeting seconds of his indecision, it became visibly obvious.

"I don't think we can go on, Robin," he said miserably. "The drought's ruining us slowly but surely. I have nothing, no prospects. Dad and I are going to finish up by walking off this place dead broke. It's useless to go on."

"Rubbish. I mean your excuses." The natural rose-pink of her face waned to leave it white and strained. "You love me. Take me in your arms and kiss me." Her voice was low, pleading.

"I don't know," he told her. "I really don't know." He reached for her, and she was in his arms and being kissed, and he was crying: "Oh, Robin, Robin! I don't know! I truly don't know."

CHAPTER 6

Desolation

IT WAS early November and every day was warm and promised heat soon to come, burning heat. This day was almost done, and no living thing would regret its passing.

Eric Downer sat on a wood case at the open entrance to the grass shed at Rudder's Well, stolidly smoking, the blue heeler lying beside him, now fully recovered.

There down at the bottom of the gentle slope stood the mill astride the well. Beyond it extended a single-line water trough, encircled by a low rampart of skinned carcases. Beyond all this the unnatural desert extended to a horizon of dun-coloured withered and stricken scrub. And on this desert, approaching the well, were the sheep, walking in parallel lines, raising light-grey dust, to be wafted away by the wind.

From another direction were coming the zombies, the animal zombies, the living dead. Only five. One short of the survivors of yesterday. They were coming along the verge of the barren plain, five cows walking with lowered heads, as though weeping for the absent bull. Their stomachs were suspended from ridged and knotted backbones, and shoulders and hips protruded like broken-off horns. The crows fluttered upward from the ring of carcases, and flew cawing with sinister mockery to meet the zombies, to flutter over them, and shriek at them to lie down and offer their eyes and tongues, because they were already dead.

Here and there along the rampart of carcases were open spaces, and the first of the cows passed through one of these, followed by the others, and advanced to the trough line. There they stood at the trough, seemingly wondering what they came for, what had happened to the bull, for now and then one less feeble would glance back in an effort to see him.

Eric saw the bull before they did. Then they lowered their heads and drank, as though to drink, after thirsting since the previous evening, was a necessary but uninteresting chore. Meanwhile, the bull was taking the pad they had arrived by. Now and then he stopped, as though pondering if he would go on, and, when moving, each leg worked as though seen in a slow-motion cinema film.

The cows took their fill of water, languidly turned and staggered from the trough, and stood working throat muscles in effort to bring up water-moistened cud to chew, consisting mostly of bark and wind-broken twigs, spiced with old and calcined rabbit bones. They failed to see the bull when he stopped once again, and sank to his knees. They did not see him try to rise and only manage to move forward on his knees, his muzzle resting on the ground and his hindquarters raised comparatively high. And they didn't see the crow that dropped to perch on the highest point of his hindquarters.

He made a valiant effort to stand, failed, merely thrusting the muzzle along the pad for another yard or two. Courage! Death was whispering in his ears. The crow was tolling the bell: caw! caw! caw! And when the hindquarters finally sank, the crow continued to toll the bell.

Taking up his rifle, Eric went to him, the heeler following. The bull barely managed to raise his head to watch him, rested his muzzle again on the ground at the man's coming, and looked upward with eyes ringed with grey dust. Eric chose to see in those eyes pleading for release.

'Tiki' they named him when they bought him from Fort Deakin six years before. He was then three years old, shining with health and ready to charge anything, be it a man or a blow-fly. Tiki! The Pointers had given them the book *Kon Tiki*, and within months old Downer, who once had driven bullocks in a tabletop wagon, could walk up to him and pull his ears, and discuss the fortune there was going to be in his progeny.

And now Eric stepped in close and patted Tiki behind the ears and pulled them. Old Tiki closed his eyes and seemed to nod, and Eric fired once.

The sun was setting, and the wind fast falling to a calm that would last till morning. The sheep were nearing the trough, travelling in seven distinct lines, each line having its leader, the links of every line one behind the other. The leaders followed a pad or path made by the sheep at previous visits to the well. To state why, would be guessing. One leader was outstanding because she had a black nose, and this evening she came on slowly, the others following, making no attempt to by-pass her to reach the water.

Eric walked among them, feeling the width of tails at the extremity of the spine, to ascertain if one was fit enough to slaughter for the larder at home. Instead, all he felt was hard bone segments. The leaders, now filled with water, turned to bunt their way back out of the press, walking on stiff legs for a little way, then waiting for followers to range up behind them. Here and there at the trough an animal went down, and Eric stood it up, and made way for it to clear the crush; same failed to remain standing, and others which were heavily loaded with water had not the strength to stand, and now never would.

The light was blazing low in the sky beyond Lake Jane when he parked the truck and carried the carcase of a kangaroo to the fly proof safe inside the cool grass-built meat house, and, having washed and brushed up, he joined his father at the dinner table.

"Anything fit, lad?" asked the old man.

"Not one worthwhile. I shot a 'roo. They're in better condition."

John regarded his son covertly, noting his mood of depression, and, to relieve it, he said, brightly:

"Had a visitor today. Robin called over."

"What did she want?" inquired Eric without looking up.

"Nothing. She brought me a little present."

"Oh!" Without a trace of curiosity. "Any news of finding Brandt yet?"

"Not a scrap."

For several seconds neither spoke, and, again covertly, John

35

regarded Eric and found that he looked not greatly different from the picture Robin had brought that afternoon. Light brown hair carefully brushed; grey eyes sombrely directed to the table; face square with a determined jaw, or an obstinate one. As always, he had changed from working togs to jacket and flannel trousers. The influence of his school was still strong.

"Did Robin have no news at all?" he asked.

"Yes. They say the river's coming down the Paroo past Hungerford."

"I mean any news about the investigation?" Eric countered impatiently.

"Don't seem to be any," replied John. "Robin says there's nothing let out on the air about it, anyway. Fort Deakin is sending away the last of its breeding ewes and its rams. Going on agistment to a place on the Darling Downs. The horses went last week, and the Pointers will have only two milking cows left at L'Albert. Jim's a bit worried about the future."

"Not the only one to be worried about the future. Nothing else?"

Old John chuckled.

"Been a fight in the abos' camp. Must have been. Fred Tonto turned up at L'Albert looking like he's passed through a mincing machine. Scalp cut open five inches, two fingers broken, only five or six teeth left of the full set, and two bung eyes he could hardly see out of. The Pointers fixed him up as best they could, and he wouldn't go down to Mindee about his fingers."

"What was the fight about?" asked Eric, looking directly at his father, and pushing aside his plate. "Over a lubra, I'll wager."

"The Pointers don't know. Tonto wouldn't say what it was about or who fought him. Anyway, as Robin put it, he's now resting at L'Albert. Nuggety Jack brought him in from the Number Ten Bore."

Neither spoke again until the meal was ended and Eric had lit a cigarette and had stared at his father for a long moment.

"We have toubles, too," he said. "We can't afford to send our sheep away on agistment, so you say, and we can't afford this and that."

"The time comes, lad, when nothing excepting agistment does any good," the old man said, firmly. "The weather patterns aren't changing to promise thunderstorms, and we won't get rain until after Christmas . . . if the northern monsoons come then."

"By Christmas we won't have a sheep left," Eric claimed.

"Or a shilling left in the bank if we spend on what isn't even a gamble any longer."

"Look!" snarled Eric, temper leashed. "Four miles out from Rudder's is scrub we could lop for feed, and a morsel of saltbush. We cart water out there to the sheep and stop that everlasting walking. Eight miles a day on empty guts would kill anything."

"Cart water! With what? All the horses we got left couldn't haul a wheelbarrow. What d'you cart water with?"

"Truck." With exploded fury, Eric crashed a fist upon the table. "I know what you're going to say. Petrol costs money. We haven't any money. We have only a couple of drums of petrol left. I know . . . I know . . . I know all about it. But I'm telling you we must do something. Damn you, I had to shoot old Tiki this evening."

John was silent for a moment before he said: "I thought Tiki would be first. It's strange that the bulls give up sooner than the cows. Better to shoot the old feller than to let him linger."

"We'll have to shoot the others," blazed Eric. "And all the sheep. What's the use of letting them walk and walk themselves to death with nothing but water in their stomachs, just to lie down and be tortured to death by the bloody crows? It can't be allowed to go on. They don't deserve slow death from thirst, torment by the filthy crows. We've got to slaughter them, clean and swift, and cash in on the skins. And have done with it all. *If* we can't cart water."

"All right, lad, we'll give it some thought. Don't be upset, now. I know it's bad to watch effort and money sinking into the sand and melting away, but it just can't be helped."

"Money!" Eric echoed fiercely, glaring down at his father. "What the hell are you talking about? I'm not thinking of money. I'm thinking about agony. You made a fuss over old Tiki, didn't you? You fussed with him when he was fat and strong. Well, I made a fuss over him this evening before I shot him. Don't you understand even now? We're holding in hell five cows and half a dozen horses, and well under seven hundred sheep. In Tiki's eyes there was accusation, and I was the accused."

Eric flung away to the back door and slammed it after him.

John sat on, his heart torn one way by pity for the starving animals and the other way by pity for his son.

CHAPTER 7

Angels in Hell

NOT TILL now did John Downer recognize, or think to recognize, the power contending for the soul of his son. To employ a phrase which explains a little-understood psychological process of change – 'The Bush was getting Eric'. As many men have a pre-disposition to alcohol, so others have pre-disposition to what might be termed the Spirit of the Bush. The degree of intelligence has nothing to do with alcoholism, and nothing to do with this absorption of a man by this Inland Australia, commonly and erroneously termed The Bush.

John was not bankrupt, and when the drought first loomed as a menace he had urged his son to return to the city and take up his career from where he had relinquished it, Eric's firm refusal, he was sure, wasn't based wholly on the fact that his father would have had to carry on with the help of only a hired hand. He refused because, having broken with ambition, he was satisfied with the life circumstances had led him to choose.

The Bush was getting Eric fast, but only now did his father think to recognize the symptoms. One: the Annual Bender this year produced in Eric no enthusiastic memories of it. Two: for the last four years Eric had declined the suggestion to take a holiday in the city and renew old school associations. Three: he seemed to have lost interest in women, typified by Robin Pointer. Four: he was permitting himself to be too greatly affected by the distress of the stock; and Five: moroseness had replaced natural gaiety. There was one more symptom yet to appear: the irresistible urge to live alone.

It was John's opinion that the best antidote for this Bush-coholism was work, rather than cold showers and changing for dinner. Work and sweat and thirst and flies and heat could bring a young man to his senses.

"I'm a sheepman," he told Eric. "I'm not one to cut their

38

throats to get rid of 'em cos it happens to be dry weather. Your other idea is better. You go out and camp on the feed and cart water to 'em until our petrol supply is finished. We'll consider the matter again when it is."

Not for many years had John spoken so firmly, nor so clearly revealed his character, which had raised him by the straps of his riding boots from a hired hand, and when Eric smiled his relief he felt hope for his future, as he thought he understood the problem.

He understood it only in part.

They went out far beyond Rudder's Well, and selected a camp site in an area where there was top feed, ie, scrub trees to lop for the leaves, and there they built a temporary trough line to be serviced by a fifteen-hundred-gallon tank to convey water from the well. The preparation occupied them three days, and then the old man in effect said: "It's all yours, lad."

And then stayed at home, telling his dead wife all about it.

The first heatwave of the summer arrived, lasted five days, and was followed by the first real windstorm. Eric trucked water from the well and prevented the sheep from passing the camp, mustering them to the unaccustomed watering place. After three days they came without mustering. And at the end of the fourth day, not one animal remained to die of exhaustion.

Despite the heat, wearing only hat and shorts and boots, Eric lopped scrub, cut posts and rails with which he built a windbreak for his tent. He cut sandalwood branches and took them to the cows. In his spare time he took axe and water bag into the scrub belts and lopped branches for the sheep to feed upon. The day temperatures were above the century in the shade, whatever that happened to mean, and the wind brought continuous dust and sometimes dust storms which blotted out the sun.

He tried to move the cows to his camping area, but they were too far gone to make the journey of only four miles. The horses smelled the water and wanted to drink there instead of going to the well, and he had to 'shoo' them away, for every gallon he could cart was essential for the sheep. Sometimes he battled with the kangaroos all night long, and in the morning, should there be a little water remaining in the trough, the galah cockatoos would congregate in their thousands and take every drop.

Every third day he filled the truck's petrol tank from the

supply inside the canegrass shed at Rudder's, and now and then measured the supply, and despaired.

Early in December Eric had visitors. He was cutting scrub when he heard them coming, and hurried back to his camp to receive them, the heeler close behind, and as lean and seemingly as sun-blackened as he. At the camp arrived the Fort Deakin station truck, and from it stepped Midnight Long and Jim Pointer.

"Making a go for it, Eric," Long encouraged, following the exchange of greetings.

"Doing what I can. Stopped the rot, or reduced it, anyway. How was the Old Man when you passed?"

"He's away down in Mindee for the inquest."

"Oh!" exclaimed Eric. "How long has he been away?"

"Five days," Jim Pointer replied. "Don't worry, Robin's been tripping out to see to the chooks and things."

"I explained to Mawby the fix you're in out here," supplemented Midnight Long, "and he found you could be excused from attending. Promised to send your dad home in good shape."

"If he can catch up with him at the pubs. He doesn't know the Old Man like I do."

"I know him better than you do, I think," Long said quietly. "Known him a long time. He'll come home when the inquest lets him, knowing what you are doing, and everything."

"Shouldn't have doubted," admitted Eric, tossing tea into the water boiling on the fire, and then wiping the pestiferous flies from his sweat-drenched face. "I've been a little hard on him recently."

"Hard times," Long said. "There's other news, too. They found Carl Brandt."

"At last!" Eric exclaimed. "Where?"

"Buried in a sandhill."

Eric lifted the billy from the fire and conveyed it to the rough bush table beside the tent, and also protected by the same windbreak. Then he said:

"Buried in a sandhill?"

"You tell, Jim. You found him."

"At the foot of a sandhill out a bit from Blazer's." Blazer's Dam was situated between the out-station and the back boundary of Fort Deakin, and had been empty for more than a year. "I was out there the day before yesterday to bring in the pump. You know the hills to the west of the Dam that look like giant waves curling over to the claypans? Saw crows at something on the claypans and went to look-see. Carl Brandt."

"Perished?" asked Eric evenly.

"Been dead for some time. Truscott says he was killed same way as Dickson. We reckon he was planted in the face of the sandhill and sand trodden down over him. Then the recent windstorms took the sand up again, and uncovered the body."

Eric, sitting on a case at the rough table, holding a pannikin of tea level with his mouth, stared with dust-rimmed eyes at his visitors. He was nibbling at cake they had brought, and unaware of the delicacy.

"There must be more," he said. "Go on. He killed Dickson, and now you say he himself was killed. I don't get it."

"No one does yet," admitted Long. "L'Albert's alive with police from Broken Hill and out from Wilcannia. Doctor says Brandt was murdered. And there was no swag and no bike with the body. Not even his water bag. Nothing but the clothed body. If his head hadn't been caved in, according to Truscott, I'd have thought he lost himself after leaving Lake Jane, and discarded his swag, then his bike, then his empty water bag, and just perished where Jim found him."

Eric pondered, his gaze moving from man to man.

"Decent of you to run out here today, what with all that and the police at L'Albert."

"Nothing we could do after yesterday. Was out at Blazer's with the police and our aborigines all yesterday. The abos have no hope at all of back-tracking. Not after nearly four months and the windstorms. So I thought we'd bring you some petrol and oil. Where will you have it dumped?"

Eric's reaction was sheer amazement.

"Petrol, Mr Long! Petrol!"

The weathered face of the grey-eyed manager wore a smile.

"I said petrol, Eric. I like a man who fights. Your dad said you must be very low on petrol, so we brought out a few drums to keep you going. Oh, don't thank me. Fort Deakin's got really too much on hand, and Lake Jane can repay when the drought's over."

"Well!" Eric brushed his eyes. "I can't thank you, not right now. Would you drop it off at Rudder's? I'll follow you there. Have to go for a load of water."

Half an hour later the station truck moved off, and, keeping well behind to avoid its dust, Eric drove his truck, the dog as usual riding beside him. At the canegrass shed they placed old tyres at the rear of the station truck and dropped the heavy forty-gallon drums of petrol on to them . . . five blessed drums of petrol and two eight-gallon drums of engine oil. Pointer helped to roll the drums into the shed, and then Eric tried to voice his thanks once more.

"Only a mere loan, Eric," Long told him. Then to Pointer: "There's a bag of stuff to leave, Jim."

Pointer climbed into the truck and handed down a sack and a wooden case, saying:

"Something from the women, Eric. Any messages?"

"Yes, plenty. Tell them I'm doing fine. Tell them . . . you know . . . just tell them."

He shaded his eyes from the westering sun while watching the truck to the paddock gate, and till it disappeared in its dust and the useless scrub beyond. He entered the shed and stood looking at the drums and the oil. Then he gazed at the case on the table and at the sack close by.

In the case was a big slab of cake and four newly baked loaves of yeast bread, several tins of butter, and a dozen eggs. There was a roll of weekly newspapers, on which was written: 'Good luck, Robin.' Eric felt like dancing a jig. The sack contained about twenty pounds of sweet potatoes, a few carrots and five cabbages, and, at the bottom, a dozen or two passion fruit – all from the river garden at Fort Deakin's main homestead. He rubbed a carrot on his shorts and proceeded to munch it. The dried product was nothing like this. He had eaten no fresh vegetables since leaving Mindee at the end of the Annual Bender.

Now with the sack and the case safely stowed on the truck, he drove it down to the well reservoir tank, and proceeded to siphon water into the large tank carried on the truck. The light of the sun was red, being sieved through the dust haze. Bluey, the heeler dog, laid himself in the trough and licked at the water. Eric stepped from his shorts and boots and joined him, and so light was his mood of the moment, he splashed water over the heeler, who pretended anger by raising a lip to reveal his teeth.

Presently the water in the tank was overflowing, and Eric flicked away the siphoning hose and replaced the tank lid. Then he saw the cows.

42

There were three only. They stood a little back from the trough, gazing without interest at the truck and the man and dog. All that were left! Just three remaining in hell. Eric closed his eyes at sight of them, turned and stepped into the truck cabin, started the engine, and then paused with his hand on the gear-shift lever. For a moment or two he stared through the windscreen at the drab and desolate plain, over which were passing the waves of red haze.

Abruptly he left the cabin and grabbed the sack and opened it.

He held a cabbage under the nose of a cow, and she took not the slighest notice of it. He broke off a leaf and lifted her upper lip and rubbed it against her teeth, and she sighed and still failed to react. He rubbed it against her teeth once again, and then held it hard to a nostril, and now her upper lip twitched, still unbelieving, and presently she took it. On her trying for more, a repetition of this dream, he held the cabbage to her nose and then lowered it slowly, as her muzzle followed it down to the ground. The others received the gift in the same manner, one falling to her trembling knees the better to eat.

The curious dog went from one cabbage litter to another, wrinkling his nose at the new scent. Eric returned to the sack beside the truck, and then portioned the sweet potatoes in little heaps under the noses of the cows. He told them they would no doubt have a slight tummy-ache, but what was a tummy-ache in payment for such a feast? In the sack he had tossed into the truck were five small carrots beside the passion fruit.

"Better get going, Bluey, or we won't even have the carrots," he said, when starting the truck with its heavy load of water.

So Carl Brandt had been found with his head bashed in. What a development! Where would they go from there? And the cows about to die, the last of them. And the sheep staggering about like reddish ghosts in a red hell of dust. But it had to rain some time, and there was plenty of oil and petrol back in the shed.

The crimson sun was setting when he arrived at his camp and the water trough, about which the sheep were gathered and loudly baa-ing a cacophonous welcome. The crows skittered away into the murk, and kangaroos, at first indistinguishable among the sheep, escaped from the press of wool to retreat a few hundred yards.

Eric parked the truck at the end of the long trough and proceeded to direct water from the tank into it. The dog ran barking to the camp, and Eric had to jump to ground to rescue sheep from being trampled in the rush of animals to drink. The dust from the cloven hooves was so thick he could barely see two yards. Once he trod on a fox lying beneath the belly of the trough, and the animal snapped at his leg. He could hear the dog barking, and shouted the order to lie down, although knowing the dog would not hear him in this din.

"Up there! Take it easy, silly! Come on now, stand and drink like a lady!" he cried to his sheep, for his heart was light at the end of this good day, which had brought petrol and oil and hope.

When at last the sheep had taken their fill and were lying down at distance from the trough, and beginning contentedly to chew cud, he stopped the flow of water, and carried the case of 'eats' to the table beside the tent. He was whistling, when from the tent stepped a girl having a round face and dark eyes, in which gleamed the light of stars.

CHAPTER 8

Eagles See Afar

JOHN DOWNER returned from the inquest in Mindee with no ill effects of alcohol, and settled into solitary existence at his homestead. About once every week Robin came over from L'Albert to fuss over him and seek news of Eric, and once during December Eric came in for a truck part and foodstuffs, and to tell of the increase of foxes that was adding to his troubles.

The days wore on to Christmas Day, which John was forced to spend with the Pointers. They ate boiled mutton and caper sauce that day, Midnight Long having travelled fifty miles to bring the fresh meat. To kill a hen was become a crime when every egg was golden. They listened to the radio broadcasts and still waited for any news of police activity on the murders seemingly now dim in history.

Jim and Eve Pointer took him home that evening, and on the way he told them that he had to go to the back of the shearing

44

shed for something and then discovered that the cross he had made and erected on the grave of Paul Dickson had disappeared. He was sure it was too heavy for the wind to blow away. It was quite an entertaining little mystery.

Two days after Christmas there began a three-day dust storm which blacked out the sun and imprisoned John in his house. At the end of it about four drops of rain fell on every square yard of country. On the last day of the year Eric came in to spend a couple of hours with him, pretending to be cheerful, stubbornly refusing to admit defeat, and admitting that the storm, plus the foxes, had cost him a hundred sheep.

And the father, who was being taught to suck eggs, loved his teacher this day.

On the afternoon of New Year's Day John was sitting on the veranda, when he noticed a number of eagles flying comparatively low far to the north. As many birds do, the eagles keep to their own defined areas unless they have a 'kill'. There was no stock in his northern paddock, and he was sure there were no kangaroos.

The area occupied by these many eagles was beyond the Crossing, and presently John's attention was held by a faint dust-mist lying close to the coarse sand. It was strange, for there was no wind, and John went inside for his hat and then walked down to the great sand bar.

Despite the dust storms, the twin wheeltracks still lay deep from one white beach to the other, and in these tracks there glinted silver and sometimes gold. Silver! Must be tin! There was a fortune in tin.

John Downer hastened down the slope and stared at the fortune in tin. He noted that all over the sand bar tiny puffs of sand dust were being blown up like the sand-puffs blown by the ant-trappers deep in their circular pits. He ran out upon the bar between the wheel tracks.

Still unbelieving, he knelt and dipped a finger into the 'tin fortune'. Water! He held the wet finger close to his eyes. He licked the finger. It was water.

Water lay deep in the tracks. It was percolating beneath the general surface of the Crossing, causing the sand to subside and thus create the dust puffs. From faraway Northern Queensland the flood rains sent water down the Paroo. Lake Jane was a backwash of the Paroo. Rain, fallen five months ago and

45

a thousand miles away, was now flowing into land burned and bleached for want of rain.

Lake Jane could be filled to the brim.

Like a child, old John Downer furrowed a ditch between the wheel tracks, and he sobbed when watching the water welling along his ditch.

PART TWO

CHAPTER 9

Inspector Bonaparte Arrives

THE MANAGER of a pastoral holding of three-quarters of a million acres isn't a social nonentity, and if he continues in his appointment for some thirty years, he isn't a fool.

The main homestead at Fort Deakin, built beside the river above Mindee, stood in an oasis of lawns and citrus trees and trellised grape vines. It had two reception rooms and nine bedrooms, and adjacent to it was the office and the quarters for the domestic staff. What with the twenty-four-stand shearing shed, the store and equipment sheds and the men's quarters, the homestead of Fort Deakin wasn't unlike a small town.

On the evening of March 26th, Midnight Long was seated at his desk in the office. There was now no book-keeper employed, now no hands other than the domestic staff, and, as there were no sheep or other stock to think about, Mr Long's managerial tasks were few, and his office confined to writing reports and keeping records.

He had just finished the evening gossip with his overseer at L'Albert when the line from Mindee asked for attention, and discarding one instrument for the other, he heard a man say:

"Mr Long? I am Inspector Bonaparte, speaking from the Police Station. I have been assigned to investigate the murders of two men in your back country, and I am wondering if I could impose myself on your people at L'Albert for a few days."

"Inspector Bonaparte," repeated Long, slowly, impressed by the voice coming from sixty miles downriver. "A few days! I believe you would be very welcome at L'Albert. Yes, of course. I thought the police had lost interest in those cases."

"In a general sense, yes, Mr Long. But I have taken over the interest, and I have been seconded to investigate from the ground up. If Sergeant Mawby transports me to your place in the morning, could I be taken to L'Albert, as the officers here are a little rushed at the moment?"

"Take you out to L'Albert in the afternoon, if you wish, Inspector."

"Good of you. And thank you. Perhaps we could bring the mail, or anything else. I'll ask Sergeant Mawby to speak."

The mail delivery being only twice a week, Long accepted the suggestion when Mawby spoke.

"Appreciate your co-operation, Mr Long. Make it an expense entry against my department. Inspector Bonaparte says he may be on the job a week or a year, so why should'nt the department pay up? Looks sideways at every penny we spend on petrol and suchlike."

"We'll all be glad to have him, Sergeant. Have I heard his name before, outside of the history books?"

"You have. By the way, in case I forget tomorrow, the wife wants to thank Mrs Long for that remedy she sent down. Seems to relieve her a little. All right, we'll leave about eight."

Once more isolated from the outside world, Midnight Long pensively filled a pipe, and with slow deliberation struck a match. Drawing towards him the Day Journal, he flicked the pages to the last entry, made this day, and added the gist of telephone conversations.

So they were going to re-open the investigation seemingly dropped. When was it the police departed from L'Albert following the finding of Brandt? Here it is. 'Body found December 9. Police departed December 15.' Now it was March 26th . . . three months. Additional three months of wind and dust storms, and shifting sand and no rain. What could a man hope to uncover now? It was six months since Paul Dickson was murdered at Lake Jane.

The strong lean fingers turned the pages. Ah! January 1st, New Year's Day. A present for John Downer, for the overflow water reached Lake Jane that day. There was a quote: 'Water, water everywhere and not a blade of grass to eat.' The pages were turned. An entry figuratively jumped at him. He read: 'Pointer reported today that Lake Jane sheep reduced to eighty-three which were slaughtered to stop expense.' The date was February 11th.

Closing the book, Midnight Long switched off the light and found his wife in the small sitting-room, where she was knitting and listening to the gossip on the two-way radio which covers so vast a network of Outback Australia.

"Have we heard about a police inspector named Bonaparte?" he asked, and without hesitation she replied:

"Yes. Elsa wrote about him two years ago. He spent several days at their place investigating a murder or something."

"Ah! Of course. I remember now. He's coming here to-morrow."

"Oh! Staying? He's a half-caste or something, I think Elsa mentioned." Mrs Long could never be precise about anyone's calling, business, or ambition. "Elsa did say he was most charming or something. Is he going to catch the murderer out at L'Albert?"

"Possibly," Long said dryly. "It's what policemen are supposed to do. Sergeant Mawby will be bringing him this far, and I'll run him out to the Pointers. They'll want lunch, of course."

"As you say. I'll tell Sarah in the morning. Er, a half-caste . . . Perhaps . . ." Mrs Long was plainly doubtful.

"I did hear Mawby address him as 'sir'."

"In that case . . . I'll tell Sarah in the morning about the extra lunch."

All doubts vanished when Inspector Bonaparte was presented the following morning. He was wearing a tussore silk suit, and Mr Long had just relieved him of a panama hat. Mrs Long found herself being bowed to, and looking, while trying not to reveal astonishment, into clear blue eyes of a dominant personality.

She was so impressed that when he departed with her husband for L'Albert she waved farewell from the veranda. The manager sensed in his passenger a new experience. Half-castes and others closely associated with the full-bloods who preferred station life to the aboriginal reserves and settlements were as familiar to him as the ordinary white stockmen. This was his first meeting with one having blue eyes, and who spoke authoritatively if a little pedantically.

"I've seldom seen the country looking worse," remarked Inspector Bonaparte. "Mawby told me you have sent away all your stock."

"On agistment. The owners are thinking of selling everything except the rams they'll keep for another six months. I don't recall a longer drought."

"And no horses at this outstation of yours." Bonaparte chuckled. "I could be destined for much walking, and I am not as young as I was last week."

"Jim Pointer will be happy enough to run you about anywhere. He hasn't much to do right now."

"Might ask him to take me over to Lake Jane. Twelve miles, I understand. You know, you should be sick and tired of policemen."

"Not at all," Long said emphatically, and added: "Owners, Government officials, policemen, all tend to break up the monotony. The Pointers will welcome you warmly."

A pause in the conversation ended when Bonaparte said:

"Miss Pointer, Miss Robin Pointer, is a very talented girl, I understand."

"An artist, yes. Plays the piano rather well, too. Convent education. Some of her pictures are memorable if a little, shall I say, macabre."

"Macabre!"

"You'll see. Very nice young woman. Trifle strong-minded, but not overbearing."

"Engaged to young Downer at Lake Jane, Mawby thinks."

"Premature, Inspector. We thought it might come to that. Could be the drought has delayed it. The young feller put up a great battle to save the Lake Jane sheep, but the drought beat him. Beat anything and anyone . . . in time."

"The aborigines, where are they now?"

"Half of them came to the river to camp. The others are living at a bore called Number Ten."

"You should try to persuade them to make rain."

"I did try," admitted the manager, ruefully. "Last year I promised them the world if they made rain, but they wouldn't play ball with me."

"I may succeed. I'll try. You took two of them to Lake Jane when Mawby was there with his tracker, and you were at L'Albert, and out at Blazer's Well, when your station aborigines were associated with that same tracker and another brought out from Wilcannia. The Wilcannia man came from Cobar, and Mawby's tracker came from Mannum. What was your impression concerning the relationship between them and your own aborigines?"

Long cogitated: "Faintly hostile, I think. Seems that when an aborigine becomes a police tracker he is regarded suspiciously, as the policeman is regarded by many white workers."

"Your aborigines, however, did endeavour to locate Brandt's bike and swag?"

"I'm confident that they did."

"Forgive me for taking the opportunity to pump you," Bony said, and Long, glancing swiftly at him, noted the smile directed to him. "I'm a born gossip, but I can keep my mouth closed. Tell me about the Downers, their history."

"Even if I were so minded, I couldn't disparage them, Inspector. Good types, both of 'em. Old John was granted his land away back in the 'thirties. Took his young wife and small baby out to Lake Jane, and they lived in a tent until he built his house. The lake was full at the time, and the seasons were good. After the war, when wool prices rocketed, they came good. Able to send the boy down to college. He did well, and was on the verge of going on to the University when Mrs Downer died. Fell sick with a poisoned hand, and tetanus took her. Tragic. Need not have been."

"It halted the son's career?"

"It did. Ambition was to become a doctor. He insisted on returning home to companion his father, who is growing old. Like the old man, a battler, but hasn't the old man's solidity of character. Hasn't the experience, of course. Old John gave him his head, and the sheep perished nonetheless. The younger generation seems to want to wear Seven League Boots. It's the same with Robin Pointer."

"Thinking of clearing out?"

"Not at all," defended Midnight Long. "What I mean is that they have tremendous confidence in themselves, but none at all in the country. These days the young 'uns want everything handed to 'em. Must have security, and all that. Certainly they don't have the compulsion to adventure like us of the last generation. Even demand what we have earned, before we're dead."

"Like everyone else, the Downers are just putting in time and waiting for rain? And their lake is full of water?"

"Feet and feet deep. Came down from Northern Queensland. And, all about, the country is like this. Even the kangaroos are so poor they aren't worth shooting for meat. I did think that under the circumstances Eric Downer might have tried to get work in a city. I suggested that his father might live with the Pointers until the drought broke. But it wasn't accepted. Like us all, they are merely squatting, and waiting."

"Then I may expect co-operation?"

"Oh, you'll have that for sure. But not after the rain comes. Better not induce the abos to make rain until it's convenient to you."

"I'll keep it in mind. Nuggety Jack is the head man?"

"He's the local chief. A long way to assimilation, you know. Canny dingo trapper and fox hunter. Does very well. Owns a car, and when he's unable to buy petrol he harnesses a couple of horses to it and they pull him around. Quite a sight. Now he has no horses, he just sleeps and waits for the rain. We're all like a lot of sick fowls."

"Any schooling?"

"Nuggety Jack? No. Has a couple of daughters, and his wife can read and write. Elder daughter is unique in many ways. Did well at school down in Mindee. Speaks nicely, too. Excellent housemaid and most intelligent. We had her at the homestead for some time, but she wasn't happy there. Then Lottee worked at the L'Albert house, but didn't remain there long. Quite a parcel when she's properly dressed. So damned hard to get maids these days. You've met our daughter, I think, Mrs Stubbs of Wonleroy."

"Wonleroy! Oh yes. I was there some time ago. She and her husband were quite charming to me," responded Bonaparte. "The case that took me there proved to be stubborn. The hardest cases to crack are those in which the aborigines are my adversaries. They have unlimited patience. So have I. It was so with the Wonleroy case. I remember that Mrs Stubbs had two delightful little children. They are growing fast, I suppose."

CHAPTER 10

The Artist and the Rain-maker

AFTER DINNER that evening they sat on the insect-protected veranda at L'Albert.

The manager had returned to his homestead, promising every facility Fort Deakin commanded, and now Jim Pointer was looking forward with keen anticipation to assisting the visitor, and so banish boredom brought about by reduced normal activity. His wife and Robin were naturally delighted by the 'intrusion', and found that Mrs Long's telephoned opinions of Inspector Bonaparte were not exaggerated.

Mrs Pointer, short, buxom, and inclined to giggling at jokes secret to herself, was ever ready to accept opinions expressed by others, but her daughter maintained reservations, especially regarding men. As Mrs Pointer was wont to say, Robin had a mind of her own, and her education, which developed her artistic gifts, had certainly given an edge to it.

She had been led to expect the unusual, and found in Inspector Bonaparte more than she had expected. The many policemen who had come to L'Albert were of the strong and silent type, with the possible exception of Constable Sefton, who was young enough, and new enough in the Department, to give back a little of what she liked to deal out. She enjoyed verbal duelling, but often found her rapier opposed to a broadsword.

"After all this time, and the drought blowing away and burying everything in dust and sand, do you really hope to find clues to our mystery?" she asked, her dark eyes bright in the white light of the power lamp.

"Not all clues are found buried in sand, Miss Pointer," he replied with a disarming smile. "Often a clue is buried in the human mind. However, clues of themselves aren't all-important. A blunt instrument is a useless thing until allied with a mental clue which is the motive for using the blunt instrument." Bonaparte paused before adding: "And what is buried can be disinterred, you know."

"Sounds gruesome," observed Robin Pointer. "Mr Long says that you've never failed yet to wind up a case. Is that true, Inspector?"

"Strong or weak, the human mind cannot shut out extraneous influences, many of which are inherited from our prehistoric ancestors. Fear of the unknown – the dark. Fear of nakedness – the light. For illustration, supposing I took up that pressure lamp and held it close to your eyes and read all your little secrets, would you not fear the light?"

"Don't do it, Inspector," implored Mrs Pointer. "Robin would certainly not like that, and I wouldn't like it either. As for Jim???"

53

"In criminal practice, of course, the investigator must rely on less spectacular methods," Bonaparte went on. "The degree of his success is related to the degree of his patience. My patience is inexhaustible. I am able to exclude from my mind the inherent sense of Time. Time is the Great Dictator ruling the human race. . . . It is the impatience of superiors, forever demanding results from inferiors, which distracts the police from pursuing a law-breaker, and thus gives him a favourable chance of escaping justice. My superiors often demand results from me, but the effect is nil, because I close my mind to their orders. I have actually been sacked several times for contemptuous disobedience, but I am always reinstated, because I have never yet failed."

"Now, Inspector, you are not being vain, are you?" thrust Robin, and the thrust was turned aside by laughter.

"Perhaps I am, Miss Pointer. I have a suggestion. Could we not dispense with surnames and titles? Everyone who is my friend calls me Bony. Even my Chief Commissioner calls me Bony. As do my wife and sons. If we were 'Robin' and 'Bony', we might contend a little harder, don't you think?"

Mrs Pointer opened her mouth to speak, and her husband smiled broadly.

"I rather like that suggestion, Bony," Robin said, eyes alight with mischief. "In fact, I think I shall like you being here. You have a mind I can challenge."

"Thank you, Robin, and Jim." Bony regarded Mrs Pointer, and she giggled.

"You may call me Eve," she said. "I'm not much of an Eve nowadays, but I used to be, didn't I, Jim?"

"Obviously. The woman tempted me." And Robin cut in with:

"If I call you Bony and am accepted as one of your friends, you will have to put up with questions I wouldn't dare ask Inspector Bonaparte."

"I might have placed myself in the position of the hunted, Robin. Is it true you are an artist?"

"Oh yes," replied Mrs Pointer. "Robin did that . . ."

"Now that we're on level ground, Bony, I'll ask my questions first."

"Very well. The next one, then."

"I think I'll save them," Robin decided. "You know, ask a question when you least expect one, because that's what you'll probably do."

"It is one of my weaknesses," Bony said gravely, and raised laughter, and approval from Robin.

In this manner passed the first evening Bony spent at L'Albert, and before going off to bed it was arranged that the following morning the overseer take him out to Blazer's Dam to look over 'The Scene of the Second Crime'.

Before they left on this excursion Bony studied a large map of Fort Deakin when it was twice its present area, and memorized place names and distances. Imprinted on his mind was a picture of this part of an immense region so necessary to see.

It was a calm day and hot, and all the orange sandhills danced a jig and beckoned from beyond the mirages. At their feet were laid shimmering lagoons of 'water'. The mulga trees were almost black, the patches of herbal rubbish were warship-grey, and only the occasional sandalwood and cabbage trees appeared to be really alive.

The windmill at Number Ten Bore was idle, and smoke from the communal camp fire rose lazily from the large mound of ash. Among a grove of native pine trees were several whirlies of bark and odd sheets of corrugated iron and hessian bags, inhabited by aborigines who appeared and stood in small groups to watch the approaching utility.

"They keep the place in order," explained Pointer. "Don't bother us overmuch, and they're happier here than at the homestead."

"The Department, through you, supplies them with basic rations?"

"Yes. They earn a little, too. Or did till recently. Nuggety Jack is a good dingo trapper. Like most of us now, they're doing nothing but wait for the drought to break.

There was no litter about the camp or the Bore, and when the overseer stopped a short distance from the pines there was no movement until he and Bony alighted, when two men and several small children advanced to meet them, followed by another who was not going to miss the conference.

One man was short and wide and powerful, and the nickname 'Nuggety Jack' suited him. The other was tall and lean, and the manner in which his hair was bunched high by a rag about his forehead indicated the Medicine Man. The third man who hurried after them was very old, but still nimble. Pointer said:

"Good day-ee, Jack! Day, Dusty! Day-ee, Fred!"

"Day-ee, Mister Pointer!" they chorused, and Nuggety Jack then became the spokesman. "Keepin' dry, eh. No sign of any breakin' of the drought. Terrible bad, it looks like."

"You're right, Jack. You trapping any dogs lately?"

"No," answered the head man, a small child clinging tightly to each massive leg.

The words were directed to the overseer, but the black eyes were concentrated on the stranger. To him Nuggety Jack now spoke.

"You police-feller come up from Mindee, eh?"

Bony glanced up from rolling a cigarette, nodded, completed the task, took time to strike a match, and slowly inhaled before replying. Then, when the blue eyes were stabbing at each in turn, he said:

"I am top policeman." Bony was wearing kahki drill trousers and shirt with black tie, his smart wide-brimmed felt hat had a pointed crown, and he knew that these people had never previously seen a policeman so dressed. He had hoped to impress them, and did so. "Are you head man here?"

"Yes," admitted Nuggety Jack, now avoiding the blue eyes.

"The Medicine Man . . . are you the Medicine Man?" he asked the lean man addressed as Dusty.

"No Medicine Man any more," replied Dusty. "We're all the same like white-feller."

"Liar," Bony calmly told him. "You have the hole in your tongue." Some of the women were now standing behind the men, who numbered eight. The men chuckled, including Dusty. "You fellers live in L'Albert country all your lives?"

"Too right," answered Nuggety Jack. "Us L'Albert abos, eh, Mister Pointer?"

Pointer nodded. He was not unaware that Nuggety Jack and his people were decidedly impressed by Inspector Bonaparte.

"I come from Queensland," Bony told them. " 'Way up in Queensland where I was born, the head men and the medicine men are good-o. They don't lie down and wait for rain to come. You dig up your rainstones and make rain, pretty quick. You make rain, and Mister Long he tell Mister Pointer to give you a five-pound box of tobacco and a full case of jam. That right, Mr Pointer?"

"That's right, Inspector Bonaparte."

The bunch of women drew closer behind the men. Their

56

presence and behaviour disclosed the distance they had come towards assimilation with the white race. Far back along the road was the point where they would not have showed themselves, or dared to be present when men were discussing so serious a subject as rain-making.

Nuggety Jack dug bare toes into the sandy ground and glanced covertly at the Medicine Man, and tall Dusty looked up at the cloudless sky, sniffed loudly and glanced at his head man. Imperceptibly he nodded.

"All right, Boss," assented Nuggety, speaking to Pointer. "We make rain, you giv-it box of tobacco and case of jam, eh?"

"That'll be it, Nuggety Jack. You get busy, now, and make it rain proper. Hi, there, Lottee! Come here, please."

Through the line of men stepped a young woman carrying a baby. For an aborigine she was tall, and, too, for an aborigine, she was pleasing to behold. Bony thought her to be eighteen, perhaps twenty, and as yet she showed no evidence of that post-maturity which comes so early to the women of her race. Her voice was low, without accent, clear.

"Yes, Mr Pointer?"

She was the only woman wearing shoes. The plain red dress fitted her well. Over the head of the naked child clinging about her neck, she looked from Pointer to Bony, her large, dark, amber-flecked eyes reflecting a serenity of mind which made her stand out from the others, who were intensely curious and excited.

"Yesterday when Mr Long came out, he said that Mrs Long was wanting to know when you'd go to the river and housemaid again," Pointer said. "Seems that Marna is going to marry that feller down in Mindee, and then Mrs Long won't have a maid. Same wages as last time, new dresses and all that. Better than here in drought time, don't you think?"

"Dad and Dusty just said they'll make rain," she countered, and now a slight smile on her face was emphatic in her eyes. She didn't believe that her father would succeed, but he was unable to see disbelief in that slow smile. "Anyway, I don't want to go to the river. Mum's poorly, for one thing, and besides, well, I don't want to go."

"All right, Lottee. I'll tell Mr Long on the telephone this evening. Mrs Long will be disappointed, I know. If you alter your mind, just say so, won't you?"

She nodded, and the infant clung the tighter about her neck. She looked at Bony and their eyes clashed. She asked without trace of bashfulness:

"Is an inspector higher than a sergeant?"

"Yes, he is. And some sergeants are higher than other sergeants. Why?"

"Oh, I just wanted to know." The smile came again to her eyes, and abruptly she turned and went back to the group of women. Her father, Nuggety Jack, now came forward, broadly smiling, and laughingly declared that they'd make rain soon, and make it rain so hard and so long that the boss would 'giv-it' another box of tobacco and another case of jam to make them stop it. Meanwhile, did Mister Pointer have 'a chew' about him?

Expecting the request, for the aborigines would cadge a chew of tobacco or a cigarette if they had a tobacco factory beyond the next sand dune, Pointer had brought a few cakes of tobacco, and now handed them round. The gift concluded the visit, and both Bony and Pointer left, amused by the happy grin on the large round face of Nuggety Jack.

Fifteen miles farther out they came to Blazer's Dam, a vast man-made surface hole at the lower end of a wide and shallow catchment area. The high ramparts of mullock no longer contained water, and under present conditions Bony thought the place utterly dreary. When eating lunch in the short shadow of the hut, he sought information.

"Are you satisfied that the aborigines honestly tried to locate Brandt's swag and bike?"

"Of course," Pointer replied, with no hint of doubt.

"Was he interested in lubras?"

"Don't think so. Why?"

"I may ask a thousand questions, Jim, and the answer to one could give a lead. Was Brandt ever stationed here pumping water?"

"He was here for four months before the dam dried out."

"Whereabouts did you find the body?"

"Away over at the foot of that sandhill, the one with the flat rooftop. We went over every inch of those sandhills, probing with iron bars pointed like spears to find anything buried."

CHAPTER 11

So Many Pictures!

"WE CALL this Brandt's Wall," Pointer said when they stood at the edge of a sandhill, some forty-five feet high, and having a sheer face so perfect that only the wind could have fashioned it. Had either made one step forward, his weight would have started a small avalanche, taking him down with it to the cement-hard, clay-pan floor of the depression.

"I am reminded of a relay race, or carrying the Olympic Torch," Bony said. "Paul Dickson broke from custody in Hungerford, just beyond the Queensland border. He made his way across country when natural waters were non-existent, and all the dams were dry, leaving only the bores at which he would obtain water. He was a good bushman, and, so far as was known, he had never travelled this way before.

"He came to the Lake Jane homestead and there he found Carl Brandt. Carl Brandt killed him, and, with his own and Dickson's swags packed on his bike, he left Lake Jane and followed the same course southward as taken by Dickson. Getting this far, someone murdered him and took over the swags and the bike, and, if we assume the same southerly course is followed by Brandt's murderer, he would eventually arrive at Broken Hill, and then proceed still southerly to Adelaide. Relay race, with death waiting at the end of each section."

"The way you put it makes it look likely," Pointer agreed.

"Carl Brandt loved dogs, remember. It appears doubtful that he would have left the Lake Jane dogs chained to their kennels, and the fowls locked in their yard without water. Had he murdered Dickson he would not have left the dogs chained, to prevent them following him. Being himself murdered, we presume that he left Lake Jane in panic haste, being menaced by the person who killed Dickson, and who caught up with him in this desolate place – to go on his escape route with the swags and Brandt's bike. How is that?"

"Reasonable enough," agreed Pointer. "It's what the police thought."

"It is what the murderer of those two men wished the police to think. What about that theory?"

The big man studied Bony's profile.

"Could be nearer the bullseye," he said. "I have a theory, too. Brandt loved dogs. He had two. When he went to the Lake Jane job he left those dogs with me, saying he'd have enough to do carrying meat from sheep that perished at Rudder's Well for the Lake Jane dogs. Supposing he expected to meet Dickson at Lake Jane, and didn't want his own dogs with him when he had to make a bolt for it? Supposing that, after he killed Dickson, a pal of Dickson's arrived and chased him over here and killed him?"

"Feasible. As feasible as the others, Jim. It is an extremely tantalizing problem – my reason for consenting to accept this assignment. How far, direct, are we from Lake Jane?"

"Eighteen miles, near enough."

"Rough country?"

"Yes. Lot of drift sand now. We'd find it rougher in the ute. Be sandbogged a lot. Anyway, the blacks and police prospected all that country for Brandt's bike and things."

"Easier going after the rain comes?"

"Yes, that's so."

"To proceed, as we think Brandt intended, from here, it would be twenty-one miles to Jorkin's Soak on the road to Broken Hill. Let's return to your homestead. I think we'll run over to Lake Jane tomorrow."

Again following the defined track between these watering places, Bony said:

"When those men were killed the weather was cool and windy. Long before that, Brandt was working here pumping water, and doubtless he spent some of his time shooting foxes and kangaroos for their skins. Long told me that he wasn't a horseman, and not a particularly good bushman. D'you think he was good enough, however, to find his way across country to Blazer's Dam?"

"Well, he must have been good enough, mustn't he?"

"Answer my question, please."

"Good enough at that time of year, but not now. The mirages now would have slewed him; they'd slew better men than he was. Why do you ask that?"

"To make the picture a little clearer. It doesn't, though."

"No, it doesn't, Bony. I don't like being beat. I was born

in Wilcannia. I went to school there before going down to Adelaide to top off. I've been working in this back country ever since, and I think I could claim to know every sandhill on Fort Deakin and neighbouring properties. I've worried over this mystery ever since it happened seven months ago, and I don't forget other mysteries before my time which have never been solved. If you solve this one, you'll be a wizard."

"Time is on my side, Jim. What Time has covered, Time will uncover. Men have disappeared, many men, since the whites took over this Land. Sandhills and sandridges have blown away to reveal a man's grave. Stockmen have ridden through a belt scrub on a hundred occasions, and find on the hundred and first a skeleton which had been lying there for decades.

"Call me a primitive, and I shall not mind. I believe in the Being which rules this Land, who watches from behind every tree and every sandhill. Respect it, and one lives to grow old. Ignore it, flout it, and it will first send you mad and then slay you. Every aborigine knows and respects it.

"This Spirit of the Land is subject to many moods. It can be benign, jealous, vengeful, and it has a sense of humour. It assisted the murderers of Dickson and Brandt by giving them plenty of time before the first body was discovered, and more time before the second lay exposed. Doubtless it has been sniggering at the efforts of every hurrying policeman, and of every white man who is alien to itself, although familiar with the physical contours of the Land it rules. . . . It will not snigger at me, but it will try my patience, my human patience, because I am with it and of it through my maternal forebears."

Following this peroration, Jim Pointer drove well past Bore Ten before he said:

"You and Robin should get along. She talks like that sometimes. I've often caught her staring at a tree or sitting on a dune and staring into space. Her mind then isn't in her head. It's away to billy-oh. You must see some of her paintings."

"I am looking forward to doing so. Is she happy here? Young women these days crave for the bright lights and social gaiety."

"We don't think it's the bright lights she wants, and there are times when I don't think it's unhappiness in love that's her trouble. She and Eric Downer thought much of each other once, but the drought has affected him badly." Pointer paused,

61

and Bony did not interrupt his thoughts. "Robin, as you will have judged, is a strong-minded wench. She's been used to bossing it over the hands and the aborigines. What with that, and because I'm easy-going, and the Boss is always very nice to us all, I believe that she has the idea that all men are still little boys. It could be that you might correct her on that point."

"It is possible, Jim. I like being placed on the defensive now and then. Exercises the mind."

"I don't. I've so many things to think about."

"This Eric Downer. D'you like him?"

"Very much. We all do. He's got guts, and he has brains. But – well, you see, old Downer sent him to a top-class public school in Melbourne, and he was about to enter the University and study for a medical degree when his mother died, and he gave it all up to come home and work with the old man."

"He regrets having made that sacrifice, if it is a sacrifice?"

"I don't think so. What I do think has happened to him is that he resents this drought which has put us all back on our haunches. Having had to abandon the ambition to become a famous doctor, he set out with a new ambition – to become a famous pastoralist. Behind it was the pride in his school. On occasions he still wears the old school blazer, and in his room are all the trophies and bits and pieces which a feller saves but usually puts away and looks at only now and then. Get my drift?"

"Surely," replied Bony. "Perhaps it's the little boy in him which attracts Robin."

"That's about it."

"She could be very good for him, Jim. Many men are happy for being mothered. And, as we know, many truly great men were made great by the women they married. I am one of them. When Marie, my wife, says 'Do this' or 'Do that', I always obey, choosing to take the line of least resistance."

"You! I don't believe. it. You're not like me."

"I don't believe you."

"Then we're both liars."

"You may be right," Bony laughed. "What I do think about your Robin and Eric Downer, from what you say of him, is that they have supreme confidence in themselves but none at all in the world about them. They'll grow out of that, if they retain common sense, and I think your Robin certainly has that.

62

This is their first experience of a real drought, and when it is well behind them, they'll be chastened and much wiser."

Later, Pointer said, obviously referring to Bony's last remark:

"Yes, a drought is a good chastener."

They reached L'Albert in time for afternoon tea, and when gathered on the south veranda, Pointer suggested that Robin show the visitor her pictures.

"Some of them are proper horrors, Bony," her mother said. "But all are really well done. The Convent Sisters wanted Robin to continue to study, but . . . I think I know why. Robins finds painting pictures too easy. Do you know anything about painting?"

"About painting, no," Bony replied. "But when I pay the piper I choose the tune."

"I should be indignant, but I'm not," declared Robin. "You'll find a lot of my stuff you won't like, Bony, but I'm sure you will understand it. Shall we go now to the Chamber of Horrors?"

"Yes, of course." He followed her to the far end of the south veranda, around to the other side of the house, where the veranda had been glassed in and curtains expertly hung to provide essential lighting. Robin drew aside a curtain, and the late afternoon sun flooded a section of the floor. On the rear wall hung pictures as though in a gallery.

"One of my early efforts," the girl said quietly, as they stood before a painting of some sugar gums in full prime, and giving shade for a group of horses. The trees and the animals were well drawn, but Bony was doubtful about the application of the colours, and said so.

"Ah! I like a candid critic," Robin said. "Now what about this one?"

There were several other pictures which, Bony decided, were of the same period, but when he stood away to examine the next one, he knew at once that this was much later. It portrayed a man in tattered clothing and running across a barren waste. The risen sun cast his shadow before him, black on the ground; and at its extremity was an open grave. The arms of the man were raised, and the face tilted upwards, as though appealing to the diabolical Beings lurking in the sky. Behind the man stood a blasted tree, in which lived a dark Being whose cheeks were distended and mouth pursed to blow a stream of fire darts

63

into the man's back. Seen dimly in the trunks of other trees were men or women all masking their eyes with a hand that they might not see.

Bony's blue eyes encountered Robin's dark and inscrutable gaze. His brows rose inquiringly, and she said:

"The Desert Spirit Slays a Man. This one is titled 'The Fool'."

Instantly Bony was recalled to Brandt's Wall. The entire background was given to a perpendicular wall of sand, so well executed that it appeared about to curl forward and crash like a wave. One third of the way up scrabbled a rabbit, and its efforts to gain the summit were clearly evidenced by the little avalanche of sand it was creating. At the base of the sandhill a dog was pawing and scratching at the sand, widening the avalanche which surely would carry the rabbit down and down. The omission of extraneous details made this a remarkable work. Bony was lavish with his praise.

"Ah! And what is this picture supposed to represent, Robin?"

" 'A Flower Suckling a Bee'. An example of contemporary art."

"Then the piper would never be paid for that . . . by me."

"Many people have no ear for music," Robin said, a slight smile about her alluring mouth. "They pay for the title."

"You should put that idea on canvas and call it 'Another Fool'. Now I do like this one. You have captured the wind in the trees and caught the sand-smoke atop that sand dune. And this one, too, of the shadows cast by dune and ridge and hump at sundown. What's on the easel?"

"You won't like that, Bony."

"Oh! Why?"

"You might resent the subject on personal grounds. I did it months ago, so there's nothing personal in it. But I would rather you did not see it."

There was a challenge in her eyes he couldn't fail to miss, and when she was aware that he saw the challenge, she turned casually aside and talked of another picture.

"May I raise the curtain, or drape, or whatever it is called?"

"Be it on your own head."

Lifting the cloth, he tossed it over the back of the canvas and stood away the better to regard it. In the centre of the picture, extending from foreground to background was what appeared

64

to be a narrow fogbank. To the right was a youth in running gear, trying to reach the fogbank, but held back by gossamer threads held by a group of white people. On the other side a nude aboriginal girl was striving to reach the bank of coloured fog, and she was held back similarly by a group of her people, who had the bodies of animals and birds. The expression on the faces of the boy and girl was of eager anticipation, and on the faces of those restraining them, either horror or despair.

"You call that?" he asked harshly.

"Kipling: 'Never the Twain shall Meet'."

"Appropriate. But the East often meets the West."

"Physically, of course," Robin conceded. "Mentally, spiritually, never."

"Kipling was wrong. You are, too. The East and the West meet in me. Why did you paint that?"

She met his steady gaze without flinching.

"I warned you, remember," she said. "I did it when a visitor told us the story of a white boy and a black girl who eloped after the parents of both had done everything to stop them. They were found lashed to a tree trunk, the tree between them. They were dead. And no one ever knew whether their murderer was white or black."

"I refuse to be depressed, or to believe Kipling. I like best that picture of the wind in the trees and playing with the sand dune."

CHAPTER 12

Bony Visits the Downers

ON JIM POINTER'S braking the utility at the house steps at Lake Jane, John Downer was standing on the veranda and Eric appeared from the machinery shed. The blue heeler recognized Pointer's smell, but was distinctly suspicious of Bony, until Bony spoke, when he ran ahead of the visitors to the veranda to welcome them properly.

"This is Inspector Bonaparte, John," Pointer said. "Out here for a couple of days or a couple of years, depending how he goes. Eric, meet Inspector Bonaparte."

"Glad to meet you, Inspector. Better a policeman than a cloudless sky," returned old Downer. "Come on in. I made a pot of tea soon's I heard you coming. Great day, if it would rain. How's things in your part of the country?"

"No different, worse luck."

No matter the time of day or night, the visitor was urged to be seated and plied with something to eat with the tea – and to hell with coffee. Coffee is acceptable only near a pub where it can be drowned with rum or gin.

"Of course," assented old John, on Pointer's suggestion that Bony stay a few days. "We're living hard these times, but we've got plenty of water, as you can see. We just knocked off for a bite to eat when I heard you coming."

"Knocked off is right," drawled Eric, shrewdly examining Inspector Bonaparte. "How are things going with you, Jim?"

"Same as with you. Nothing doing, Eric. Only hard smoking and waiting for rain. It'll come soon. The Inspector persuaded Nuggety Jack and Dusty to dig up their rainstones and make it."

"They did?" asked John, suddenly serious.

"They said they'd get to work," replied Pointer. "We offered 'em a five of tobacco and a case of jam. They'll 'sing' for rain for a week for that."

"They'll 'sing' for a year, and then claim they made it," Eric contemptuously asserted, and his father vociferously backed the aborigines.

"Tell you what, lad," he said, sternly. "The abos never start 'singing' to their rainstones unless they are pretty sure rain isn't far away. They're cunnin' enough for that."

"What's your opinion, Inspector?" Eric asked, grey eyes slightly appraising. Bony, who was now feeling what he thought was racial hostility behind the probing grey eyes, and remembering what Pointer had said of Eric's cultivated school background, replied with a counter.

"I don't know a great deal about the aborigines. You see, I was found when a small boy beside my dead mother, under a sandalwood tree. It was said that my mother was killed for giving birth to me. Anyway, I was given over to a Mission, where the Matron reared me and saw to my education. What with High School and the University, followed closely by a police career, I never had the opportunity of joining in sacred tribal rituals I would have had, had my father been black."

"Oh, you went to Uni., did you? What Uni., Inspector?"

66

"Brisbane."

"Lucky fellow! Did you gain a degree?"

"Bachelor of Arts."

"Again, lucky fellow." Now approval was plain to see on the younger Downer's face. "Glad to have you with us, I'm sure. We need a bit of brainwashing. In the best sense, of course. How's everyone at L'Albert, Jim?"

"The sinus troubles have let up on the wife during the last few days," answered Pointer. "The Boss said when he brought the Inspector that Mrs Mawby has been pretty crook with sinus, and so's several others down the river."

"I knew something would happen when they put disease into the rabbits," snorted John. "Stand's to reason you can't loose germs and things into animals without us humans getting it. I never heard of anyone having sore eyes and noses and sinuses before they loosed the myxomatosis."

"Myxomatosis is non-communicable to humans," Eric said a little stiffly.

"That's what the quacks tell us," John argued. "I seen Mrs Mawby with it and a couple of kids in Mindee, too. Same symptoms exactly. Don't you reckon, Jim?"

"Could be. Still, the stuff did reduce the rabbits before the drought got to work and killed off the lot. But they'll come again, and then the quacks'll loose something else on 'em, and we'll get rotten bones or white blood, and the quacks will blame the fallout."

The old man was becoming heated, and Bony said:

"You aren't really barracking for the rabbits, are you?"

"Course I am. Country's not the same without the rabbits. Who wants the rabbits cleaned up? The rabbits are the poor man's food. While there's rabbits no working man and his children need starve in Australia."

"Anyone listening to you, Dad, would think you were a working man," Eric said, soothingly.

"Well, I am at that."

"No, you're not. You're a full blown pastoralist with no ruddy sheep to your name. So close your clapper."

The ire faded from the old but bright hazel eyes, and slowly a smile spread over the dark face marked so vividly by the white moustache. Humour rushed to the rescue.

"A pastoralist! Me! Crikey, so I am, Eric. To hell with the working man. What d'you say, Inspector?"

"I say you two would be most obliging did you call me Bony. Everyone else does."

"Suits me, Bony. Anyway, you're welcome to stay as long as you wish. We've only two bedrooms here in the house, but the hired hand's room can be made comfortable. Can you play cribbage or poker?"

"Both, reasonably well, I hope."

"Then we'll all be set. No money, though. We play for matches."

An hour later, when local gossip dried up, Jim Pointer left, and the Downers carried out the promise of making the room at the end of the machinery shed truly comfortable.

"Do what you like," old Downer told Bony, and Eric added:

"Take you anywhere you want, show you anything you want to see. We've still a little petrol left for the truck."

"Now, Eric, you fix that room, and I'll show Bony around," importantly ordered John, and Eric smiled behind his back and winked, and said he would convey the visitor's baggage to the guestroom.

"When Eric fixes it, you'll be all right here," John said, as they stood at the open door of the room under the same roof as the machinery shed. Then the old man showed Bony exactly where the body of Paul Dickson was found, moving a saw bench to give a clear view.

"I have seen the official photographs," Bony said. "By the way, you never did find your son's hair or the watch?"

"Neither. Not even the cards those locks of hair was sewn to by my wife, rest her soul. I still get headaches thinking on what happened here."

"We'll have to talk it over quietly some day, John. I am far from satisfied with the picture as you saw it when you and Eric came home from Mindee."

"Me neither. Long time back, though. Terrible lot of dust and sand blown over any clues since then."

"The abos might make it rain," Bony said. "Rain might wash the dust off a lot of clues, mightn't it?"

John Downer brightened.

"If those black bastards do make it rain! Did they seem real anxious to get down to it?"

"Yes, I think so. After the Medicine Man made up his mind. We stopped at Bore Ten on the way out to Blazer's Dam, and they weren't about when we passed on the way home. It's

68

probable they had already gone off to dig up their rainstones."

They were walking towards the shearing shed, which Downer proudly wanted to show, as a shearing shed, with its pens and yards and interior plan, is more complicated than a house.

"What d'you reckon?" he began. "Think the abos can make rain?"

"I do think that by observing signs they tend to make believe their rainstones when properly 'sung' will bring rain."

Bony was shown around the shed, and was informed that John had built it with Eric's assistance, and Eric had installed the machinery for the two-man stand, and that the wool press had been purchased in Sydney.

"Another feller and me shore twelve thousand one year," claimed John. "That was before Eric came home for good. Three years ago him and me shore close to nine thousand. Now we got nothing."

"How many did you have at your last shearing?"

"Fourteen hundred and nineteen they tallied. That was last June."

"You put all the shorn sheep out at Rudder's Well paddock?"

"Yes. Feed around here and up north had gone."

"Did you muster them for a count after you returned from your holiday last September?"

"Took a rough tally at the Well. About a hundred died when we was down in Mindee. Why?"

"Unlikely, then, that Dickson, with or without Brandt, was engaged in sheep stealing?"

"Not likely. Don't think."

"Dickson was buried where?"

"I'll show you. Out back of the shed."

The grave was marked only by rails nailed to four posts.

"The police wanted to put him in the wife's plot down front of the house," John said. "Eric wouldn't have it, and I wouldn't of had it either if I'd been handy, which I wasn't at the time. You see, the wife's plot is only big enough for her and me. I don't much like this, though, just planting a man with nothing said over him. So I read a bit of the service, and put up a cross, and weeks after, when I came here, the cross was gone.

"I didn't find it, and so I put up these rails, and afterwards I asked Eric about the cross, and he made no bones about

69

telling me that the feller was a criminal and wasn't entitled to a cross. What do you think?"

"Ticklish question, John. However, I think I'm on your side."

They moved on round the rear of the house, and the hen yard, and then John said:

"We mustn't take notice of Eric, Bony. The lad's had a real tough time with the sheep and the drought and all. It's his first drought, you understand. Terrible lot of his mother in him, rest her soul. She was a real woman, if you understand what I mean. Couldn't bear to see suffering. Eric was always closer to her than he's ever been to me.

"Mind you, I got nothing against him. We been good cobbers always. But watching animals die, and not being able to do much about it, sort of tossed him off balance. He battled hard to save the sheep. I knew he hadn't a hope, but I gave him his head. It made him very touchy. Sort of broke him down. He didn't used to be like he is."

"At the end of the drought, and when you have to build up the flocks again, he might regain his old self, John."

"I'm hoping so." John paused, then said: "Feller has to be hard, don't you think? Has to be able to shut his mind off what can't be helped. I've had to do it. So have others."

"One has to be philosophic," agreed Bony. And now they were at the road gate in the fence enclosing the entire homestead. "Tell me, when you and Eric returned from Mindee to find the dead man, was this gate open or closed?"

"Closed. I remember having to get down to open it for the truck."

"It isn't closed now. Was it usually closed then?"

"Only at night time to keep the dogs from going away hunting. We had three then, you know. The chooks was always out and about the place during daytime, but was locked up at night to save 'em from the foxes. What's on your mind?"

"It's said that Brandt chained the dogs to prevent them from following him. He'd just killed a man, and he wouldn't delay getting off with his packed bike. He had to leave by this gate. Why did he delay to close it?"

"Crikey! Yes, why?" echoed John. "No man would muck about with a gate when in a tearing hurry to get away from a murder."

"Doubtless Brandt's mind was at the time most unsettled," Bony pointed out. "No one else came here after he left and before you and Eric arrived back? Could there have been someone?"

"No one from L'Albert," replied Downer. "They'd have noticed something wrong."

"No one came over from L'Albert, John. I asked Pointer that. You haven't any other near neighbours have you?"

"None at all. Besides, if anyone had come, they'd have banged on the house door, and, finding no one at home, would have slipped a note under it saying they'd been. Don't have no strangers, no travellers this way, Bony. Only a feller like Dickson who escaped custody."

CHAPTER 13

A Page of History

WITH THE sun far down the western sky this calm hot day, Lake Jane was like a marcasite in a setting worthy of a more precious jewel.

The surround of orange sand dunes was unmarred by the print of man or beast, and had been caressed and moulded by the wind to fantastic shapes, majestic outlines, and to the delicate curves of the rose. Here in playful mood the wind had buried a tree up to its first branches, making it appear as a bloated cabbage, and there had lifted another to stand absurdly on its splayed roots, through which a steer could gambol.

As Bony walked down the slope to the lake with only a towel about his middle, he might have been the First Man to venture into Eden before it was made ready for him, and although his bare feet made not the slightest sound, he felt the urge to walk tiptoe. On the hard white beach, the towel cast aside, he flexed his arms, expanded his chest and tightened his stomach, and felt like shouting, and dared not. Starkly nude, he was one with this starkly nude land.

Several herons stood at the tip of a tiny spit, as though looking at themselves in the mirror of the lake. A party of teal ducks were as tiny black warships on a metallic sea. With the water to his chest, Bony was tempted to splash some of it

71

upon the nude land, and tell it to clothe itself with green garments.

"A wedge of swans came down here when I was taking a bathe," he told his host at dinner. "The water is alive with tiny orgasma. Is there any fish?"

"Plenty, but as yet very small," answered Eric. "Too small to hook, but they'll grow fast."

"Fish!" chortled old Downer. "Last time the Lake was full, we caught fish up to seven and eight pounds. Ducks! They laid eggs everywhere, even up the trees. Go out any time and fill a four-gallon tin with 'em."

"Meanwhile we have to live on kangaroo," Eric reminded them. "I'll have to run out to Rudder's this evening. Care to come?"

"Yes, I would. Four miles by the map isn't it?"

"You've seen a map?"

"In Jim Pointer's office."

"That's a good one. A bit short of four miles actually."

"I take it you are still running water into the trough at Rudder's Well?" Bony questioned. "For kangaroos?"

"Yes. Strangely enough they aren't about Lake Jane. They got used to watering at Rudder's, I suppose. It might be that, being accustomed to water slightly brackish, they don't like this Lake water. Anyway, I can always pick up one out there after sundown."

"Well, you'd better get going. Sun'll set in half an hour," the old man reminded his son.

Seated in the truck with the dog riding behind, Bony remarked on the boat he had seen moored to a stake. Eric grinned, saying he had built it in great haste when the down flood over the Crossing cut them off, and that he was building another, for something to do.

"According to the Old Man, and I don't doubt him, Lake Jane will become a paradise for fishing and shooting, and the 'roos will gather around in thousands, and the rabbits will come and multiply in millions. That'll please Dad. Mind you, he has a lot in favour of the rabbits. When the rabbits are thick, the dingoes and the foxes and the eagles don't attack the sheep and lambs."

"You had trouble with the foxes?"

"In the end it was the foxes that really beat us," replied Eric. "I was carting water and holding the sheep on scrub, and the ratio of foxes to sheep became something like six to one. When a sheep died at the trough at evening, nothing of it was left next morning, bar tufts of wool, and bones scattered for yards."

Talking thus, Bony watched the track unwinding before the truck; the passing trees and scrub, areas of bare red earth, low dunes of windswept sand, and, at one place, spinifex to which still adhered feathers from the fowls Eric had jettisoned many months before. Save for a bird or two, there was no living thing to be seen, for reptiles would freeze to immobility on sighting the vehicle.

The general impression was of drabness and aridity, until they came to a wide belt of tea tree, a ramose shrub growing to a height of from seven to ten feet, and having but little space between each. The small and bright green leaves offered pleasurable contrast, as well as the sense of intimacy gained from a forest.

Half a mile beyond this tea tree belt, there appeared above the general scrub the tops of two sandalwood trees, their slender leaves reflecting the sunlight with the purest green of any in this world. On coming to them, Bony could not fail to admire their straight trunks and unspoiled shapes, and it was as though the poor scrub trees stood back also to admire them, for the ground on which they stood was level and paved with untarnished red sand.

And immediately afterwards that impish, malicious, mocking Spirit of this Land, of which he had talked with Jim Pointer, fired a bolt to destroy the complacence into which he had fallen. There was a blurr, a technical error in that picture of the sandalwood trees.

The doubt was rooted in Bony's mind when they arrived at the gate to the Rudder's Well paddock, and during the next few minutes doubt was frustrated by the interest the place would arouse in anyone coming to it across this arid country. All about the long trough were a hundred-odd kangaroos, and, upon the grey ground, slivers of dull red slipped and dodged – the shapes of foxes, come early to quench thirst which could not wait until darkness. Over all whirled and screamed the birds, converged upon this particular place, when within a short distance was a lake of fresh water.

Eric parked the truck in front of the grass shed, saying he would take the rifle to the trough limit and select his kangaroo. Bony decided to wait in the truck with Bluey. Watching Eric walk with deceptive unhurried haste to the far end of the trough, where he waited for the animals to regather, Bony summed up this young man. Knowledgeable, self-assured, a battler, stubborn and intolerant, Eric had not his father's resilience to pressures exerted by prolonged drought. A dashing cavalry officer, but not the commander of a besieged fort!

Eric fired once, and the birds rose with deafening cacophony, and 'roos and foxes raced away, leaving one kangaroo to tell of good marksmanship. When he came for the truck, instead of carrying the carcase to the vehicle, Bony asked:

"Was it away out across the plain that you held the sheep on scrub feed?"

"Three miles out. I don't want to live through that experience again. And yet I'm glad that I did what I could do for the sheep, and for the cows and horses that died out here."

Bony helped to lift the kangaroo to the truck, and noticed how cleanly it had been shot through the head. It was young, and its condition was surprisingly good.

There were facets to this young man which Bony liked, and facets, too, which he understood.

The sun had set when they left Rudder's Well, but the light was still strong when they passed the two sandalwood trees, and although he strove to detect what was wrong with this picture among so many others, he failed. Doubt of its balance, its perfection, was brought by the Spirit of the Land to doubt the doubt.

But Bony was akin to this Land, and too close to its presiding Spirit to permit a doubt of the doubt to influence him. If anything were to be doubted it was 'Did the flaw in the picture of those sandalwoods have a connection with the investigation?' It was remotely possible. The white man, seeing a stone lying on a bed of roses would not bother to reason why; but an aborigine who saw a spider dead in its undamaged web would spend time and thought on that flaw in the picture. Spiders don't die naturally in the web.

The course of the relay race with death, as Bony had described the two murders, almost certainly passed by Rudder's Well to Lake Jane homestead, following the defined road. Thus anything amiss in that section had to be examined by one who claimed never to have failed.

Opportunity came the following afternoon when the Downers were working on the new boat. Bony slipped away and, carefully avoiding the road, came to the clearing at the side farthest from it. Here he sat in the shade of a needlewood tree, or rather its trunk, for the narrow leaves give but scant shelter. The natural clearing was approximately a hundred yards across, and nothing grew in it bar the two sandalwoods. The wind had swept the area clean of dead leaves and small twigs, leaving only the heavier tree debris, immediately below the trees. Sand particles blown against them proved that the prevailing recent wind had come from the north-west.

The match he had used to light a cigarette he placed in his shirt pocket, and when done, the cigarette butt went into the same receptacle. Removing his boots, he moved around in his socks, to lessen risk of being tracked.

At the side of the road and in the approximate position he had been when on the truck, he gazed searchingly at the scene to locate the flaw. He could see the large sticks used by a pair of eagles to fashion their nest at the very top of a dead box tree beyond the clearing. They would have caused a decided imbalance had they built amid the leafy branches of the sandalwood. This applied, too, to the position of the bag, made by the social caterpillars, suspended from a dead branch of a near-by mulga. Its being there was natural; it was certainly not the flaw he sought. There were many other similar objects, but not one to create the imbalance.

It is a fact that one cannot see the wood for the trees. The flaw was eventually found close to his feet, and only two yards off the track.

It was a branch torn from a tea tree shrub, the smaller subsidiary branches intact. The leaves had long since withered and vanished. The wind had partially buried it with sand, proving that it had been there for some considerable time. There was no reason to account for its presence at this place.

The were no tea tree shrubs growing here, and the nearest was the wide belt of them half a mile nearer the homestead. So what! Well, why was the stone lying on the bed of roses?

The wind could not have brought it, because it was much too heavy. It would not have fallen from Eric Downer's truck, because the truck was fitted with sides and tailboard. It would not be carried by the aborigines from camp to camp for firewood. It is used sometimes to thatch the roof of an outhouse, but this material had not been so used at Lake Jane, nor at Rudder's Well.

75

A small problem unworthy of a white man's attention!

It was obvious that the wind had not brought it, and equally plain that it hadn't been used by anyone as a fly whisk. Used by someone! For what purpose? It could be an efficient eraser of footprints. Were that so, then what had been the motive?

Without expecting a result, Bony, from various positions on the circumference of the clearing, crouched to gaze angle-wise across the ground, seeking for any irregularity left by the action of the wind. Meticulous attention to detail, unlimited patience, and unbounded curiosity received their reward from the ancient Spirit of the Land who had tested him.

The wind had patterned the surface, and by bending low he was able to see the pattern etched by shadow cast by the miniature ridges. The pattern was perfect save in the middle of the clearing, where an obstacle had contended with the wind.

Standing over it, he could not detect the slight flaw on the wind's pattern, and he sought for the cause with the toe of a socked foot. Thus he felt a hard object a fraction above ground level, and with his hands exposed the end of a burned stick. More delving brought to light pieces of charcoal, unburned ends of small sticks, and ash.

Why bury a small fire in this country when ground surface was so denuded of grass and herbal rubbish?

History was written on this page of the Book of the Bush. Someone had made a small fire in the centre of this clearing, and then dug a hole beside it and buried the residue. With that tea tree branch he had erased his foot-tracks, tossing the branch aside when he completed the task. For this purpose he had brought the branch from another place, viz. that belt of tea tree.

CHAPTER 14

Patience Rewarded

IT was not unlike trying to read a serial story backwards from the instalment one picks up by chance. Someone had come to the sandalwood clearing, carrying a branch of tea tree with which to conceal his purpose. He had burned something of importance to himself.

The belt of tea tree crossed the road nearer to Lake Jane

by half a mile, and Bony reached it by keeping parallel with the winding track. As estimated, it was a hundred-odd yards in width, and he proceeded to examine that section of it extending on the same side of the road as was the sandalwood clearing. The bushes, for they cannot be classed as trees, were unaffected by the long rainless period. Their shadow was black on the red, windswept ground, and here and there a branch had been broken by the wind. The vital branch must have come from this belt.

Again in stockinged feet, Bony wandered among the forest of tall bushes seeking to read on this page of the Book of the Bush a word to connect it with the writing in the clearing.

There were the prints made by a fox, roughly like a four-leaf clover, and the animal had crossed the belt since the last high wind, and had evinced no interest. Then he detected a dingo scratch where a dozen or more bushes grew unusually close. The markings of the claws were old, and those of the pads had long ago been erased by the wind.

A dog doesn't obey a nature call save at a place used by another dog, although, of course, there always has to be a first dog. Now a first dog will invariably succumb to habit at a place or object which had attracted its interest by way of his nose. It was not, therefore, by chance or luck that Bony was interested in these close-growing bushes.

The centre of them provided a natural bower where the sunlight was masked, the air cool, and the wind, when it blew, would be defeated. The floor of the bower was covered deeply with tea tree tips, now dust-dry, grey and brittle. The alignment of the tips proved that they had been gathered by human hands and placed carefully in position to form a couch or mattress.

The tips had not been slashed or broken from the walls comprising the bower; they had been gathered and laid some considerable time before, when the branch found at the clearing had been severed from the parent bush. Another detail Bony learned was that the tips had not been lain upon after they had lost their leaves.

Why make camp here? There was no water nearer than that at Rudder's Well. If the tea tree branch at the clearing had been used to erase footprints, and he was confident that had been the purpose, then it could have been employed here for that purpose. A secret camp was indicated.

Why the secrecy? The aborigines would have no reason to form a secret camp, and it would be most unusual for them to take the trouble to pick bush tips and make so perfect a sleeping mattress. An aborigine would merely light a fire on the lee side of a bush, and lie down between it and the bush and sleep as comfortably as he might in a featherbed. In fact, he would damn the featherbed.

It was a puzzle to delight Inspector Bonaparte. He crawled over the mattress of twigs, quartering it, finding nothing. He wormed his way in and among the arboreal walls, hoping to find a clue in a spent match, a cigarette end, anything to give a lead to the camper; and found nothing. He prospected out-side for a fire-site, a food tin, even a meat bone, even another buried fire-residue, and was disappointed. So he proceeded all over again, starting with the mattress, unarmed with a magnifying glass, because his eyes were as good.

Patience is seldom unrewarded. He found his clue outside the bushes forming the bower. It was entangled by a bush spur, all the seven hairs of it!

The owner! The hairs were black, and similar to those found clutched in the hand of Paul Dickson. The owner was probably a blackfellow, but it could be Robin Pointer, for her hair was similar in colour. But then so was the hair of half a million other women down in Melbourne and Sydney.

Further clues were necessary to create a picture from the dusty past, and although Bony spent another hour, he was not further rewarded. He might have spent yet another hour, had it not been advisable to return to Lake Jane before the curiosity of the Downers was fiercely aroused.

So widely did he circle that he came to the Lake well beyond the Crossing, and then followed the narrow white beach re-maining above water. The house windows were reflecting the sunlight, and smoke was rising from the single chimney. A hundred yards from shore Eric was diving from the boat, and after his long afternoon walk, Bony decided to fetch his towel and swim out to join him.

He was, however, given no time, for when he was nearing the house old John came to the veranda and banged on a tray to call the 'hands' to dinner.

"Go far?" he wanted to know when they sat to dine on kangaroo steak and dehydrated vegetables.

"Feel as though I did," Bony replied wryly. "Wish I had

78

a horse. Like Richard of old I'd give my kingdom for a horse."

"Horses are as scarce as kingdoms in these parts right now," Eric pointed out. "Where did you prospect?"

"Beyond the Crossing, to see the country that Carl Brandt headed for when he cleared out. The map says it's eighteen miles to Blazer's Well, and from what I've seen of the country today it would be a very hard eighteen miles."

"You're right there, Bony," agreed John. "Some of the roughest country out that way. Hard on a man afoot, and harder still on a man pushing a loaded bike, let alone trying to ride it."

"Brandt couldn't have known what he was in for when he left here with his bike loaded with two swags," Eric averred. "He knew the Blazer's Dam end, and all about the Dam, because he shot 'roos and trapped foxes in his spare time, but he didn't know this end. I've always said that somewhere on that trip he planted his bike and the swags where they won't be found in a hurry, either to travel faster to reach the road at Jorkin's Soak and thumb a ride down to the Hill, or because he knew he was being trailed, and found he could travel faster without the bike."

"Perhaps too much emphasis is placed on the theory that he was trailed by someone and killed in revenge for killing Paul Dickson," temporized Bony. "He could have been killed for the bike and swags where his body was found. His murder could have no connection with the murder of Dickson."

"That could be," agreed John. "But there was no one in that section of the country at the time. There was no stock, and no water."

"What of the aborigines? Some were camped at Bore Ten, were they not?"

"Yes. Nuggety Jack and his mob were at Bore Ten, but if you knew Nuggety Jack you'd know he and his crowd wouldn't murder for a bike which anyone at L'Albert would recognize."

"They couldn't sell it to anyone," supported Eric "There was not one stranger at L'Albert to sell it to, even for a plug of tobacco. You have to take into consideration all the conditions at that time, and they were then no better nor different from what they are now."

There was impatience in Eric's voice, and more than a hint that he was bored by the subject. Bony thought he could be excused, for discussion of one subject for seven months would bore anyone. He said so, and Eric met him with:

"I know it's your job to investigate these murders. I don't mind in the least answering questions on topography, climatic conditions, people. But to talk about what might have happened, when no one knows what did happen, gives me the willies."

"But Bony, nor any detective, wouldn't get far without arguing this and that," John said, placatingly.

"I agree with you, Eric," Bony told him, "It's impolite and unwise to talk shop at dinner, in any case. Theorizing takes us nowhere. That picture there: did Robin Pointer do it?"

"Yes. About four years ago. Her best period, I think. Eve Pointer calls her studio the Chamber of Horrors. Did you see her pictures?"

"Mrs Pointer suggested it, and Robin took me to see them," Bony replied, and John Downer felt easier in his mind.

"And what is your opinion of them?"

"There was a picture of horses standing in the shade of sugar gums I liked very much, and another of the wind in the sand dunes I thought exceptional. Mind you, I have no knowledge of technique, and the rest."

"Nor have I, but I like her work, or some of it. Others I detest."

For the second time this evening Eric's grey eyes became hard bright discs in his dark face, and once again his father was troubled.

"She has certainly caught the Spirit of the Land in her picture entitled 'Desert Spirit Slays a Man', and there is something of it in the one called 'The Fool'. The one on her easel I thought particularly well executed, although it did come close to home."

"Oh, what was that?" asked Eric.

" 'Never the Twain shall Meet.' "

"I don't . . . I haven't seen that one. What's it about?" Eric was perplexed and surprised. "Had she just finished it?"

"It didn't appear to have been done recently." Bony described the picture in detail, and as he proceeded, the fingers of Eric's left hand began drumming on the table. When he paused, Eric would have spoken, but Bony continued: "I fear that I took the whole thing a little personally, when it wasn't intended, as I quickly realized. Robin said that the idea for the picture came from a visitor's story."

Eric's fingers still beat the tattoo, and John asked if Robin had related the story.

"Yes, she did," answered Bony. "It appears that a young white boy fell in love with an aborigine, and despite warnings and pleadings of their respective parents, they eloped. They were found bound to a tree, both dead, and it was never known which side killed them."

"I must have been the visitor, 'cos I told her that story," John said. "I told her that story a couple of years ago."

"You never told it to me," Eric burst out. "You never said anything about telling her that yarn."

"Damn it, Eric, why lose your temper? Nothing to tell. It happened years and years back. I remember it sort of came to me on the spur of the moment."

"I told her that Kipling was wrong, anyway," Bony said, quietly. "I told her that the East often meets the West, and that the East met the West in me."

Eric sighed, and the fingers ceased their drumming to permit striking a match for a cigarette. Then he said, with spurious calm:

"Did you see her picture called 'Surrender'?"

Bony shook his head.

"Pity. Great work of art. Shows a lamb in the talons of an eagle. The eagle has its bloody beak deep in the lamb's stomach, and the lamb's head is fallen back and you know that no longer can it feel pain in the death kind enough to come for it. Did you see the one called . . ."

"What about calling it a day, lad?" asked John, and Eric stood and glared down at them.

"Did you see the one called 'Interest in Anatomy'? There's seven crows on a tree looking down at an eagle on the ground. The eagle has in its beak the entrails of a horse. It is walking away, pulling the entrails from the horse yard by yard. And the horse has its head raised and is looking at what the eagle is doing, and in the horse's eyes you can see . . . Great God! What do you see in the horse's eyes!"

Eric pounded the table, and old John stood, his hazel eyes like the blacks' rainstones, and his mouth like a dingo trap.

"I tell you that I hate that girl when she does that with paints," shouted Eric. "And I could hug her, too, for putting on canvas the Truth, for tearing the blindfold from our eyes, so that we see ourselves as the wretched, tortured animals see

81

us. When she showed me those pictures, those frightful, those utterly truthful pictures, I wanted with all my might to strangle her. Instead we clung together, and I kissed her, and in her kisses I sought for understanding and sympathy for me, for the horror I felt, and there was no sympathy, nothing but desire. I tell you both that Never the Twain shall Meet . . . not the twain we are."

Panting with emotion, Eric sat and buried his face in his hands. After a few moments, during which his father and Bony were silent, he said more calmly:

"You two clear out to the veranda. I'll clear up the dinner things. Sorry I lost grip."

Bony nodded to John Downer, and the old man followed him to the veranda. He sat and began cutting chips for his pipe, and Bony stood at the rail, and gazed out over Lake Jane, now painted crimson and black and silver by the sunset sky, and changing the ring of sand-dunes to purple. Neither spoke as Lake Jane appeared to sink lower than the sheets of colour, and then Bony said, excitement causing him to drawl:

"Come here, John, and tell me if you can see what I think I see."

Against the glory of this desert sunset sky, myriads of black dots were arranged in broad arrow heads.

"Birds," whispered John.

The arrow heads swiftly became larger, yet did not alter distance between them. There were others behind them, like stepping-stones to the Evening Star.

"Pelicans!" cried Downer and, rushing to the house door, shouted: "Come on out, Eric! The birds are coming home. Come out and watch."

Eric came to stand beside his father, and what he witnessed drew despondency from him, and renewed the enthusiasm of youth. The pelicans were descending on a long glide, occasionally a bird using its wings to maintain exact position. They were approaching as arrows aimed at the very heart of Lake Jane. John said, gripping Eric's arm:

"There's always the good things, lad. Just look! The birds are coming home at last."

Squadron by squadron, every wing taut, the fleet passed in review, the last of the day's light gleaming like ivory on the majestic prow of every ship.

CHAPTER 15

Flotsam and Jetsam

THE 31st of March was a day to be recorded and long remembered. It began by bringing to John Downer a restlessness of mind, which drove him to suggesting they all pay a visit to the Pointers at L'Albert. Eric voted in favour, and Bony against, as he had thinking to do and reports to write, and clothes to wash.

Bony had the clothes on the line and letters written when the Downers left shortly after nine, the old man saying on leaving:

"There's bread in the crock and cold 'roo in the meat safe. The place is all yours."

Bony took him literally. Having seen the truck vanish in scrub beyond the Crossing, and smoked a cigarette whilst watching the massed pelicans at the far end of the Lake, he entered the house and glanced into old John's bedroom. The heavy brass and iron double bed was neatly made. There was a marble-top washstand bearing an ornate ewer standing in a matching basin, and which, doubtless, had not been used since Mrs Downer died. There were pictures on the walls, and these interested Bony. A photograph of Mr and Mrs Downer showed her as having been taller than her husband. Her eyes and brows indicated a placid temperament, her mouth and chin a strong character. Beside it was the portrait of Eric, done by Robin Pointer.

Eric's room was as neat as that of his father. Here were pictures of him at school: one of form grouping, one of the football team and another of the cricket team, in both of which he was prominently placed. He was then not as darkly good-looking as he had become. In a picture of the school cadets he was a sergeant, slim and stern.

When cutting himself a lunch of bread and meat, Bony was feeling in his own sons the pride that Downer and his wife must have felt in Eric. Today Eric was a victim of the drought, which had found him without the armour worn by more resolute and less sensitive men, but when drought was defeated he would regain poise and confidence.

Having written a note saying that, after all, he chose to tramp to the back of the run, and that he would take the heeler with him, he filled a canvas water bag and before noon was boiling water at Rudder's Well for lunch tea.

On this hot and windless day he had walked four miles, and again wished he had a horse to carry him across the man-made plain beyond the mill to the distant scrub line dancing in the heatwaves. It was comparatively cool sitting in the shade of the canegrass shed, when from the heat stepped the Devil to tempt him.

Why tramp out into that sea of heat and blinding mirage? Why not relax here in the coolness of the shed? Later, when the sun is setting, you could stroll comfortably out there to Eric's one-time windbreak and tent camp. Why, you could camp there tonight, look around in the early morning, and be back at Lake Jane before the sun becomes really hot again.

Then the Devil blew up in smoke and flame, and an Angel stood at Bony's side, saying: What of that spill of black hair you posted off to Superintendent Pavier by the Downers this morning? What of that place where you found the hair? What of the dead tea tree branch, and the little fire so carefully and yet, paradoxically, so carelessly buried? Would you have risen to become Detective-Inspector had you gone on strike because you felt lazy on hot afternoons?

Emus stalked to the trough and rested on the ground to drink. A belt of even cloud at great height was slowly moving down from the north. Credit, however, to whom credit is due. It wasn't the promise of shadow which caused Napoleon Bonaparte to take up his water bag and gunny sack, call to the heeler, and plunge into the fierce sunlight.

The flies were infuriating. The cloud-belt would never cover the sun. There would not be any reward for this senseless tramping about. Yet no man knows what the next minute will bring to him, what he will see should he climb to the summit of a sandhill, how he will react should he feel a bull ant in his trousers.

It was, of course, that Angel; the Devil had been doing so well, too.

Three miles out in the shimmering heat, Eric Downer had built his two sheep camps, the second necessary when the scrub had been lopped and the bush eaten out at the first. To visit both meant following the sides of a triangle having its

84

apex at the Well, each side approximately three miles long. Thus it was an hour of solid, withering walking to reach the first camp.

The bones were there. The bones of the windbreak and the bones of animals whitened and scattered as though each of ten thousand foxes had sought to dine in seclusion. There was no shade, for the scrub trees had been lopped and felled, and the ground sprouted only the stumps.

Having taken a few sips of water from his bag, and poured half a pint into the dented crown of his hat for the heroic Bluey, Bony smoked one cigarette before concentrating on every foot of the camp, on every inch of the skeleton windbreak, and finally on the enlarging encirclement, until convinced there was nothing of interest.

The base of the inverted triangle was clearly marked for him by the truck transporting Eric's equipment to the second camp. He was well on his way along this second side when the cloud shadow reached him, and the burn of the sun on neck and arms was lifted.

"Rain! Rain, my foot!" he told the heeler. The cloud mass was so thin that the underside was barely darkened. In the semi-shadow, the dismal stretches of withered scrub appeared even more desolate, and the occasional gum and box trees were positively repellent now they had no shadow to offer the dead earth. By comparison the red sand country was virile.

The light car or utility truck gave something like a shock. The vehicle had either been coming from Rudder's Well, or going to it. Investigation convinced Bony that this cross track was older than the track of the truck he was following, and, knowing that the latter had been made about twenty weeks back, he guessed the light track had been made about two to three months before it.

It would have to wait, for the second camp was just ahead.

The second camp offered an appalling picture of a lost battle. Here, too, Eric had built a windbreak for his tent and table, and here were the tent-pegs and the pole, and the legs of the table cut from the scrub and needed no more.

The posts and rails of the windbreak were still in position, but all the leaves of the tree branches laced to it to temper the wild westerlies were blown away. The foxes had licked and played with and scattered the heap of food tins. The sparse herbal rubbish, the debris of lopped scrub, even the windbreak

– everything had caught tufts of wool from dead sheep whose bones were weathered and strewn over a great area.

A few yards in front of the windbreak, the remains of the camp fire were still evident beneath the cross-stick from which cooking utensils had been suspended over the flames. On a wire hook was an almost new billycan. Leaning against a stump was a long-handled shovel, which, like the drinking trough, had yet to be collected for removal to the homestead.

The trough was corkscrewed and drunken. Under it the foxes had burrowed great holes to seek the moisture deposited through leaks. They had clawed and burrowed for chance food scraps about the table legs, and where Eric's stretcher had stood within the tent. The wind had teased the summits of their hillocks but failed to blot out the story of their hunger.

As though to heighten impressions, the cloud mass passed from the sun, continuing to revolve as it travelled slowly southward. Upon the grey earth the white bones gleamed whiter, each one representing a scar on the mind of a man.

The signs, and there were many, gave the picture of a man frantic to leave a scene where finally he had been defeated, with no loss of honour. He had slain the last of his sheep and skinned them, tossed the skins on to the truck, added the skins previously taken from sheep that had perished, collected his stretcher, bedding and personal possessions, not thinking to add a shovel, a billycan and perhaps lesser equipment. Abruptly surrendering, leaving the field to the growing horde of foxes, he had turned his back to horror, but had been unable, figuratively, so to turn his mind.

Bony was walking back to the camp from his farthest circle when he entered a shadow, and for the second time saw a vast cloud mass. It, too, was slowly revolving, but travelling from east to west. Reaching the camp site, he lit a fire and poured a little of the water from the bag to his billy for tea, and then recalled that the first cloud mass had travelled from north to south.

Bony sat with his back to the stump which had carried the tent's ridge-pole, and shared the remains of his lunch with Bluey. Thereafter he smoked two cigarettes, and the smoke rose straight in the windless air.

To his right were the legs cut from the scrub to carry a board for Eric's mess-table, and, as elsewhere, the foxes had burrowed and scratched in the hunt for a chance-missed bone or bread scrap. There was an object lying between the legs, probably a small bone, and Bony's eyes were tired and his brain wearied by white bones, large or small. The shadow departed, and the glare returned, when the very whiteness of that small bone again demanded his attention, because it was where it ought not to be.

The cloud wheel was passing to the west, and the sky behind it was deep and pale blue. Cloud masses did not usually behave like this, but the interest in this phenomenon was slight in the balance opposed to that secret camp amid the tea tree, and the concealment of the fire in the sandalwood clearing. Bony stood, and almost at his feet was the little white bone. He picked it up. It wasn't bone. It was plastic. Half an inch long; it was a delightful replica of a white horse, having an attachment ring in place of a saddle.

It appeared to be a talisman such as is carried by a man. Or it had graced a bottle of a well-known whisky, or perhaps come from a woman's charm bracelet. Was there a charm bracelet in the Treasure Chest at Lake Jane?

About the place where the table had been erected, Eric's boots would have reduced the top soil to the fine grey powder in which the foxes had fossicked and chanced to raise the white horse to the surface. A man's actions are concentrated about a table, and would also be concentrated about his stretcher bed. With the tip of the shovel blade, Bony methodically tilled those two tiny fields.

A sieve would have served so much better, but the shovel brought to light two shirt buttons where the stretcher had stood, and, where the table had been, he salvaged a small tin containing tobacco and papers, and a hair comb. The comb was curved, and the teeth long. And no man uses a curved comb.

If the little white horse did not fall from a man's watchchain, then possibly it had been attached to a woman's charm bracelet. In these days, what man wears a chain attached to a pocket watch? With his hands, Bony scarified the powdered ground and found nothing more of value.

Tired and triumphant, this patient man sat and smoked and pondered, the dog lying at his side with head on forepaws.

"Where, friend, is this investigation going to lead me?" he said aloud. "A woman's comb and a white horse, found here in a man's camp?" Had Robin Pointer visited here with her father? Quite often she did drive alone to Lake Jane, and she could have run out here to see Eric. "I shall have to dig into that, Bluey, old cobber. The affair between those two could have been much deeper than the respective fathers appear to think. Now what is the matter?"

The dog had stood, and was as immobile as the tiny white horse. Bony stood and gazed to the point indicated by the dog's nose. Two kangaroos were passing the deserted camp, loping easily and without haste. Then the first stopped, swung himself round, and lifted to his full height to stare back whence he had come. The second 'roo stopped and also stared back, the two as motionless as Bluey.

That they had been disturbed, probably by a dingo, was proved by the line of progress. They had come from the north and were running to the south before stopping to look back. The sun said it was after five o'clock, at which time they would be making towards Rudder's Well from the east to the west. Like the cloud wheels, they were behaving abnormally.

"Sit!" ordered Bony, and Bluey sat, but continued to watch the 'roos, that were several hundred yards' distant and unaware of the man and dog. They were surely interested in something, for they continued to sit balanced on their tails.

Through the wreckage of the windbreak Bony peered for minutes and could detect nothing likely to have alarmed the kangaroos. He expected to emerge from the landscape of bush rubbish and scrub stumps the dingo, or dingoes, which had frightened them. But nothing moved. When first one kangaroo went to ground, and then the other, he decided they were confident they were no longer being hunted.

Whatever the cause of their uneasiness, it might be found when returning along the base of the triangle to the point where the tracks of the car or utility cut it. The shadows of this battleground were lengthening, and the sun said it was after six o'clock, when Bony and the dog left the place with no regret.

Bony saw nothing, and Bluey scented nothing of what had disturbed the 'roos. On coming to the track of the car, they then turned towards Rudder's Well when following this track, and quickly Bony desisted from even guessing its age. The vehicle had been driven erratically, but the driver's purpose had been to avoid patches of low scrub, gilgie holes or soaks, and steep dry watergutters.

88

The wheel-tracks crossing a claypan were barely discernible, as was a slight indentation midway between them which halted Bony. This was oblong in shape and four by five inches in size, and could only have been made by a wheel jack. The driver here had had to change or mend a tyre.

The dog wasn't interested. He was definitely interested in a patch of scrub which bordered this wide claypan. Recalling the incident of the kangaroos, himself seeing nothing suspicious, Bony 'sooled' the dog forward.

The magnet could be a fox or a dingo, a kangaroo, even a man. Bony was led to a gilgie hole amid the scrub trees. The hole should have been wide and deep. It was now filled to ground level with cut scrub, leafless and dead and months old.

"Sool 'em, Bluey," Bony pleaded, and the dog nosed about and finally went down under the scrub by a hole made by the foxes.

The result was comical. Some twenty-odd foxes raced from various holes and departed at speed, several stumbling over tree debris which their eyes, unaccustomed to the sunlight, failed to see. Then Bluey emerged, and that part of his upper jaw naturally white was now black. With ash.

Why would someone light a fire in the bottom of a gilgie hole, and cover the site with scrub branches?

As though he had not trudged all day in the blistering, airless heat, Bony proceeded to fling out of the hole the dead scrub, and himself to sink foot by foot to the ashes at the bottom.

He grazed an ankle on the frame of a bicycle from which the tyres had been burned from the wheels. Without thought for his clothes, he delved among the ashes and found belt and strap buckles, the porcelain mouthpieces of two water bags, the toe and heel plates of what once had been a pair of boots, a safety razor and the blade of another. There were three billy-cans and two small fry pans, as well as other oddments without which no man carrying his swag, or strapping his swag to a bike, would travel.

Having tossed the branches back into the hole, and taken time off to roll a cigarette, Bony and the dog continued on their way to Rudder's Well and Lake Jane. The day was nearly over. It had been a wonderful day after all, thanks to the victory of the Angel, and what now comprised the contents of his gunny-sack. The little white horse reposed in a tight pocket.

The ground was being claimed by advancing Night, but

Day still ruled the western sky with its colours of red and mauve. The bars of red rested on a range of dark mountain summits.

The moon rose behind Bony, huge and lemon, and the moon-man puffed and huffed a little wind to cool the back of Bony's neck and arms. And Bluey became quite excited by the scent that little wind brought to him.

PART THREE

CHAPTER 16

The Sweetest Murder

THE DOWNERS spent the evening reading the latest acquisition, of days-old newspapers and journals. They spoke seldom, being weary from reaction of a day of gossiping, and the excitement of visiting, and, too, disappointment in not finding Bony at home. His letter saying he intended going off on a tramp was understandable, but the postscript intimating that he might not be back until the next day mystified both.

There were other matters tending to cause depression. One of the first subjects opened at L'Albert was whether the aborigines were persisting in their efforts to make rain. The Pointers could give them no information, and after lunch Robin and Eric went out to Bore Ten in the station utility. They returned to say that the men were still away singing over their rainstones, the women and children not being permitted to be with them. Both were moody, and the elders mutely agreed that the afternoon hadn't been one of loving courtship.

The diverse course of the cloud masses passing during the day had not escaped anyone, and at sunset, when the Downers arrived home, they believed the clouds on the western horizon to be another cloud wheel.

Now their finite world was silent, save for the occasional rustle of paper, until John said, trying to be cheerful:

"Ah! What I always said, lad. Listen to this. The myxomatosis, the wonder-virus which a few years ago was killing rabbits by the million, is, like the sack line, on the way out. Those that survive the first attack of myxomatosis pass their immunity to it to their offspring."

Eric grunted non-committally, and his father continued the observations with tremendous satisfaction in his voice. "Kill off the rabbits! What a hope! What a mass of brains, thinking they could kill off our Australian rabbits. Why, when the last man is blasted from the earth the rabbits will still be running around licking up the radiation. Scientists, they call themselves! I'm only a common old working man, like the feller who owned Glasgow Town, but I always knew the rabbits would beat 'em. If we'd had the rabbits for the foxes and dingoes to hunt, we wouldn't have lost our sheep."

"Dry up," pleaded Eric, continuing to read.

John completed reading the article in silence, when he had to burst forth.

"I always said the germs would get us humans, and they have, lad. There's Mrs Pointer even today complaining about her sinus, her nose stuffed up and her eyes running . . . just like the rabbits before they died, running around blind. Scientists! Oh no, they say, myxo can't affect humans. Oh no! What have they done? They've reduced the rabbits, temporary, and the farmers and squatters have grown more sheep. For what? To pay more and more taxes for our politicians to travel around the world on cigars and champagne. I always said . . ."

Eric flung down the papers. "I said 'Shut up,'" he snarled, and left the kitchen. The slam of his bedroom door wrote more than a paragraph. John frowned, shrugged, blew out the table lamp, and with heavy heart groped his way to his own room.

He was sure he wouldn't sleep, but he fell asleep within minutes of getting into bed, and it seemed that immediately he was asleep he was awakened by a voice on the veranda.

"Hey, there! Here's a lotion for sore eyes. Come out at the double. Awake ye sluggards!"

John recognized Bony's voice. He heard Eric moving in his room, and, without bothering to slip on his old gown, he opened the front door and stepped on to the veranda. He was then conscious that Bony stood at the rail, with Bluey beside him, but interest in them was snuffed out by the giant striding towards Lake Jane.

The moon at zenith sailed a sea of translucent purple in which the stars were tiny specks of phosphorescence. The moon at full shed its splendour upon a celestial glacier resting on an ink-black base. Deep within the glacier, like wire gold in white quartz, lightning lazily flickered, and the staccato bark of thunder was stifled by the steady roar of rain meeting the ground.

Extending from the south-west to the north-east, the cloud-bank slowly heightened and slowly advanced, the brilliant white of its summit in sharp contrast with the purple sky.

Nowhere did it break open and reform, or dissolve and re-appear. At no point did it threaten to topple forward to engulf its ebony base.

Thus did it march upon Lake Jane. It advanced to the moon, seeming to rise ever higher than the moon, and, to the fascinated men, seeming to draw the moon down, that it and the cloud giant meet face to face, resulting in the inevitable destruction of the moon.

About the house was a vacuum silence, beyond which the water-birds continued their ceaseless conversations. They were completely unafraid, and betrayed no sign of excitement.

The distant shoreline of dunes did not gradually fade into the black base of the storm. Its disappearance was abrupt. Then the ebony wall was upon the water, carrying its mighty burden of dazzling ice as a barge might convey a load of sugar.

"The windows!" Eric shouted, and sprinted into the house, where he was heard, slamming down window after window. Neither Bony nor old John moved. They were possessed by the feeling that Lake Jane, the house and themselves were rushing towards the cloud-base, and swiftly the relationship of themselves with the cloud-base, and the cloud with the moon, was changed by the shifting angles. The cloud-base lost entirely its appearance of solidity, and the cloud its appearance of ice and snow. The moon became sick with apprehension.

The near shore-dunes entered the darkness, and the darkness was speeding up the slope when the moon was gobbled up by the monster. And the men retreated into the house and barred the door.

Eric had lit the table lamp, and they stood about the table, waiting. The house was utterly silent. The roar of the deluge deepened as it approached, rose to deafening cacophony when it fell upon the corrugated-iron roof.

Nervous tension gripped Eric. He could feel the house quiver, and could imagine it being swept down the slope into the lake. Bony tossed his gunny-sack to a chair, and it gave forth a sound of tinkling metal. Rarely had he watched the approach of a storm when the moon was in such favourable position in a clear sky. Old John must have put on spring-heeled boots. He was jig-jogging on his feet. His hands were beating the air as though the thunderous roar was music and he was conducting. The incongruity of his striped pyjamas was surely banished by the expression of sheer joy, as he listened to the noise on the roof to detect any variation of the tune.

The Era of Creeping Death was passed, and the Era of Bounding Life was begun. There were children of three and four years who had never seen a raindrop, and who, on running outside in the morning, screamed in terror on seeing water running over the earth.

"He's breaking up," yelled John Downer. "Hark at him! He's breaking up, lads; he's bustin' his guts." At last he permitted himself to believe that the drought was truly ended. Now he might have been barracking at a fight. "Go on, you beaut! Sock it into him."

The house continued to stand, and Eric leaned over the table and turned down the smoking lamp-wick. Bony rolled and lit an alleged cigarette, and then suggested something to eat. This brought Eric to balance, and he nodded, and turning to the stove, pushed kindling wood into it, tossed in a dash of kerosene, and stood back to toss in a lighted match, which ignited the vapour in the still hot interior, and caused the stove to shudder from the explosion.

Eric draped a cloth over the table, and Bony went to the bench sink and turned the tap, from which water hadn't run from the roof tank for six months. At first it spouted mud, and then poured clear water upon his hands, and, seeing it, Eric laughed from hysterical relief at this further proof of the drought's end.

Having dried his hands on a bench cloth, Bony raised the window above the sink, and the air which flowed into the house, and all about the three men, caused each to breathe deep into expanded lungs. It was unbelievably aromatic. John rushed to the window, exaggeratedly sniffing. Then he turned about and rushed to the veranda door, and disappeared into the void beyond. They could hear him shouting.

The clock on the mantel said it was forty minutes after midnight when Bony sat at table and gratefully ate kangaroo chops and damper bread, and, having poured tea into enamel mugs, Eric sat opposite again to listen to the rain on the roof and beyond the window and door.

"Bluey is in the house somewhere," Bony shouted. "Any bones for him?"

"Oughtn't to be inside," Eric asserted. "Not allowed inside." He whistled, and, after hesitation, the dog appeared from a front room, the picture of guilt, and fear of the elements.

He was patted and given a bone and he lay on a rug and chewed without relish, fearing to be turned out.

Abruptly the thunderous roar on the roof stopped, and the lesser noise of rain pounding the earth drew away and softened.

"That was terrific," Eric said. "Must have given three inches."

John appeared at the veranda door. "Come on out and listen to it. Every creek and gutter is running a banker. Come and listen to the birds talking about it."

Eric impatiently waved refusal and to Bony said:

"You must have been on a fair-sized tramp. Must have smelled the rain coming."

"I was out in the middle of Rudder's when I saw the rain-clouds just after sundown," Bony gave, knowing the rain would have washed out his tracks and filled the gilgie hole and washed away all that sinister ash.

"Learn anything?"

"A little. I found where two swags and a push-bike were burned. I brought the metal relics back with me. The bike was too buckled to wheel, so I left it."

"Are you referring to Brandt's bike, and his and Dickson's missing swags?"

"It's unlikely I would be referring to anything else."

"No, I suppose not," Eric said. "Are you sure it was Brandt's bike? Any proof of the swags belonging to him and the other feller?"

"The bike can be identified, I've no doubt. The swags . . ."

"Yes, yes, of course it can. But . . . hang it, Bony, it doesn't add up. You found this stuff out in the middle of Rudder's Paddock, you said. Why out there? You know what I mean. Why take it out there to burn it?"

"I've always been better at asking questions than answering them," Bony side-stepped. Eric was about to speak when a single raindrop pinged on the roof, and both listened to hear the next. It came a moment later, and was followed by another. The rain began again, and John appeared, to shout, unnecessarily:

"It's on again, lad. We're goin' to get some more. Come out and listen."

"All right, we will in a minute," returned Eric. "Where-abouts was the fire, Bony?"

"This side of a line between your two sheep camps. There

95

were the tracks of a car or utility near by . . . extending beyond your camps to the north-east."

"I saw no light tracks."

"Understandable, Eric. You were driving a truck when your mind was on sheep problems. I was on foot."

"Yes, that was so." Eric regarded Bony pensively, brows knit above eyes both alive and puzzled. The rain became heavier on the roof, and John again appeared to call them to listen to it. "Let's see the stuff. Wait, I'll clear the table."

"When you came home from your holdiays last September, did you see tracks of a car or utility on the road to Rudder's?"

"No," replied Eric, shaking his head. "Might have been had we looked hard enough. But we were thinking about the sheep and what could have happened to the mill since Brandt had cleared out. Brandt disappearing like that didn't give anyone cause to look for strange tracks. We must agree to that."

"That would be so," Bony said quietly, and then, as Eric had removed the cloth, he emptied the contents of the sack on the table. "D'you know what kind of razor Brandt used?"

"Blade. Saw him shaving one morning. H'm! That could be it."

The old man came in, and this time came to see what interested them. He wanted to know what it was, and poked a finger to separate the items. He asked where it was found, and wasn't keenly interested on being told. They could see him repeatedly 'cocking an ear' to the rain singing its carols on the roof. He was vibrant with energy.

"Put it away till the morning, and come and hear the birds talking, and the water dropping down the spouts and running over the land, and sinking inch by inch into the ground to germinate all the seeds."

He went out again, and Eric made a cigarette before speaking.

"My theory could be right after all. Fellers came down from the north, did their killing and went north again, burning the bike and swags on the way. What do you think?"

"You could be correct," Bony agreed. "The only other person I know of who owns an old car is Nuggety Jack."

"Wasn't him," Eric defended. "I do know that at the time Nuggety Jack hadn't any petrol and was then driving horses harnessed to his car. He couldn't have driven his horses about this place, and at Rudder's, without Dad or me seeing proof of it."

"The rain is going to keep on all night," Bony predicted. "Well, that leaves the Pointers and their utility."

Eric's eyes blazed with anger. "What the hell do you mean by that?" he asked with voiced raised.

Bony looked up from the task of returning his treasure-trove to the sack. His eyes were steady and dark in the light of the lamp.

"A person yet unknown drove a car or utility across Rudder's Paddock at about the time of the murders," he stated. "He burned the bike and the two swags in a gilgie hole and covered the lot with scrub. We agree that the vehicle wasn't owned by Nuggety Jack. Nuggety Jack is therefore eliminated. Another possible is Jim Pointer with his utility. I said 'possible', not 'probable'. We will eliminate Jim Pointer. We could, but won't, consider Midnight Long and his utility. Eliminating this one and that one is no cause for anger."

"I'm sorry. I wasn't following your drift." Eric began the making of another cigarette, and this time his fingers were active. "What about . . ."

He was stopped by his father, who came to grip Bony by the arm and shake it whilst glaring across the table at Eric. This time he really 'went to market'. He was now the Tribe's Old Man, the Assessor of men and events in the Balance of Wisdom.

"You and your ruddy murders!" he yelled. "What the hell's the use of yapping over two silly murders like them? Come on out and listen to the birds telling each other and chortling over the sweetest murder of all time, the Murder of King Drought."

CHAPTER 17

Earth Smiles Again

OLD MAN DROUGHT was dead, battered and bludgeoned by little drops of water. The beaten Earth, ravished and scared, bedraggled and weary, conceived, and the womb prepared to give forth its fruit.

The rain guage at Lake Jane failed to register, but in an

empty kerosene tin the storm had deposited water to one-third its capacity. Thus the Downers were able to estimate that the fall was nine inches. It came in the best of all seasons, at the end of summer, and weeks before the cold winds of midwinter, and occasional frosts.

All men were immobilized. Local creeks carried water for the first time in years. Frogs that had lain dormant for years deep in the ground emerged from the sodden earth and skipped and croaked and courted in the short time before the invasion of the birds took place. The cicadas bored their way up from the depths, creaked and groaned whilst beridding themselves of old bodies and taking on new ones, plus wings. The bardee grubs came from treetrunks and up from tree-roots to split their skins and emerge as great winged moths the size of a man's hand, and from every termite's nest myriads of winged insects poured like smoke from miniature volcanoes to take part in the nuptial flight. The day following the night of deluge was the day of the winged insects. The birds came on the second day, darkening the sky above Lake Jane, blotting out sections of its far shore, churning its surface by their ceaseless landings and take-offs. In mid-morning of the third day, John Downer called Bony to see the leaping grass and herbage, and the next morning every sand dune every sandy area, was changed from red to green. Within one week the wind was waving the tops of fields of grass.

"In a way a drought is a blessing," John said one afternoon, when he and Bony were lounging on the veranda. "If there weren't any droughts you wouldn't get a bull-dozer through this country for the jungle, and you wouldn't cut your way through it without meeting a snake every other yard, and being chewed up by the leeches and lice and fleas, and other vermin. Droughts do keep this country clean."

"Positively," agreed Bony.

"She's come good again, eh?" chortled John, the glory of this rebirth reflected in his eyes.

"How right you are, John," admitted Bony, knowing that seldom has modern man come so close to this Ancient Land as John Downer. Since the rain, John's mind had been cleaned of the past with all its grim struggles, its pain and hardship, its murder of animals and men, and its ceaseless assault on his faith.

Beside them stood Eric, silent and morose. Now he said:

98

"We have miles of ground feed, and floods of water, but no sheep, no cattle, no horses. You work like hell and you lose the lot. You build up again, and what you build is levelled."

"We'll get some sheep, lad, and a horse or two, and cows, never fear," John said cheerfully. "Look, I still have four and ninepence, plus a bit, in the bank. We had better be doing something about restocking. Have a word with Midnight Long about it. When d'you think the truck could do the Crossing?"

"Tomorrow. The water stopped running yesterday. Local floodwater. If a major flood comes down the Backwash, then it might be a year before the truck could be got across. Depends how far north the rain went."

"You might take me with you on the next trip to L'Albert," Bony suggested. "I've finished here for the time being. Been a pleasure to be with you."

"Been a pleasure to have you," Eric said, and his father backed him with energy. "Think I'll try for a duck or two, and have a look at the Crossing. Might take a few birds over to the Pointers. We owe them a debt the size of Lake Jane."

Eric left, and a moment later they could see him strolling down to the lake with his gun, and dog at heel.

"Like the country, he'll come good again," John said. "Times have been rough on him and all. He's a good lad, and he gave up a lot to stay home with me."

"Might marry and settle down, eh?"

"I'm hoping. So's Jim Pointer. Make a good pair, wouldn't they?"

"Yes, I think they would," agreed Bony, adding a proviso. "They're much alike, John, and yet have traits which could amalgamate to give steady happiness to both. What each needs is a little of the sunshine of prosperity and renewed faith in a future. We all need that, of course. Has Eric other interests beyond sheep?"

"Yes, I think so," replied John. "Still takes a great interest in his old school. Runs down to Melbourne every year to attend the Old Boys' Annual Dinner or Dance and what else." The old man knocked the ash from his pipe, then said: "You know, before this drought mucked him up, and it did muck him up because he was all right before it started, he was thinking of veterinary science, and aimed to go down for a course in Melbourne. But the slow grind of drought got us both in. One thing in his favour is he don't take after his old man on a bender. Likes a drink or two and pub company and all that, but don't keep going like me."

"This rising generation has different ideas and other outlets for spending money, don't you think?"

"That's so, Bony. Yes, that's it. Give Eric's generation six whiskies and they keel over."

"Talking about him and the cursed drink, how did he put in his holiday with you in Mindee? Not much social life there? No cinema or dance hall, is there?"

"Nothing like that. He didn't hang around Mindee all the time. Went over to Broken Hill to see some friends. Plenty of amusements and such like in the Hill. Pretty good dancer, Eric. Can sing a bit, too. Never forgets the old man, though. Always remembers when it's time to collect him. You been to the Hill, of course?"

"On several occasions. I cannot foresee where my next assignment will take me."

The two reports from Eric's gun sent ten thousand birds rising like dark vapour upward from Lake Jane, and in thirty seconds innumerable flights of duck streaked over the sand dunes as though to give the swans and the pelicans better space for their slower take-off. By the Crossing, Eric waited with gun ready, and Bluey was bringing to shore a victim. The gun spoke again, and Bony saw the duck collapse and fall quite close to the man.

"He's a good shot, John."

"Good at all sports. Bit of an all-round champion at school. Even got into the newspapers. The printing about him we put in a little book, and the book's in the wife's Treasure Chest. Hope I get that watch back with his picture in it. Sure it wasn't burned with the swags?"

"I'm sure," answered Bony quietly. "Are you sure that nothing else was taken? A ring? A necklace? A bracelet?"

"All the things are there bar the watch and those two cards of hair."

The ducks were skittering down upon the lake, and the bigger birds appeared in no hurry to return. Eric came back with four plump black ducks, and with the information that the Crossing would bear the truck the next day.

"Should have gone in the boat. What say you two lend a hand getting it down to water? We could roll her down without too much trouble."

"You refer to the new boat?"

"Yes. Completed her yesterday. The old one I've broken up for the iron lining. We'll want that."

"We'll give it a go, lad."

Although much superior to his first effort at boat-building, the new craft was heavy for its length, through lack of proper materials. It was nicely shaped, having a square stern and sharp bow. It was flat-bottomed and fitted with two thwarts.

The effort to get it down the slope to the lake-side was harder than expected, but eventually the craft was launched, and at once began to fill with water.

"Crikey!" shouted John. "Wants more caulking. Anyway, the seams will swell and stop leaking."

Eric laughed, and Bony couldn't fail to note how attractive he was when in a gay mood.

"Come on! Up with her to the beach before she sinks," Eric commanded. "She'll be all right when she has the floor plug in. I forgot to put one in."

They managed to drag the waterlogged craft part way up the beach, and Eric departed for a baler and a plug. Returning with both, he jammed the plug and baled out the water, and a second launching was effected. A rope held the boat fast.

"Rides good and light," exclaimed John. "Better than the old one. Big enough, too, for three to go fishing. We'll have to rig some tackle."

The boat was drawn to shore and was found to be watertight.

"I'll get the oar and give her a trial," Eric said, and they waited for him to bring it.

"A new interest," Bony said, regarding John with raised brows.

"Yes. I reckon new interests will crowd in now the drought's busted." Affection and pride shone in his eyes. "Blood'll always tell, Bony. His mother was strong-minded, and once Eric makes up his mind there's nothing wrong with Lake Jane and the country in general, he'll do well."

Bony's nod of agreement was slight, and a moment later Eric appeared with the single oar. Slipping off his boots, he pushed the boat out, climbed in over the bow and, standing, deliberately rocked it. He shouted when it rode perfectly, and, using the oar over the stern and feathering it, he propelled the boat out from the shore.

"Done the job better than I thought, Bony," murmured

John. "Was always particular. Everything always has to be done just right. Yes, good job considering he had only sawn timber and sheet iron to make her with. I showed him how to curve the ribs, and he took it up in a flash."

That night was the most carefree evening Bony spent at Lake Jane. Eric was almost gay, and his father happy in what seemed to be the son's rejuvenation after so many severe trials. They played cribbage till midnight.

The next day the truck could never have been driven to L'Albert had it not been for John's piloting. He displayed an uncanny knowledge of the comparatively hard surfaces, for to have followed the usual track would have meant being bogged time and again. As it was, the twelve miles to L'Albert occupied four hours.

To Bony, L'Albert was never so populated. From a veranda Eve Pointer waved to them, and Robin met them with smiling welcome. Jim Pointer was in conference with a party of aborigines outside the store, the men, women and children dressed as though for church at a mission station.

"Well, it is nice to see you all," Robin said, looking steadily at Eric still sitting behind the wheel. John wanted to know how much rain had fallen at L'Albert, and was told ten points over ten inches. Eric wanted to know what the party at the store was about, and the shadow in the girl's eyes passed when she replied:

"The rain-makers have come in for their rewards. And all their dependants. You knew that Dad promised tobacco and jam if they made it rain. And how they made it rain! Well, get out, do. Lunch will be ready in a few minutes."

"You don't really believe all that tosh, do you?" asked Eric, mockery in eyes and voice.

"Don't see why not," defended Robin. "Bony suggested getting the aborigines to make rain. Dad agreed to give them jam and tobacco if they did. So they dug up their rainstones and rubbed them with their magic stones, and 'sang' them in a secret camp. And then it rained."

"And then it rained, so why the argument?" supported John. "Come on. Let's get out. I'm cramped sitting here all day. You're looking fine, Robin. How's your mother?"

"Better since the rain," she replied. "We've started our garden again, and Mother's been absorbed by that and forgotten all about her sinus."

Lunch was a hilarious affair, although the cold mutton was tough and the portion of potatoes for each was very small. Eve Pointer was famous for her pastry, and her pie made of dried apricots earned her sincere compliments from the visitors.

After lunch, old John, with an eye for future labour needs, accompanied Eric and Pointer to the aborigines' temporary camp, to talk with Nuggety Jack, and, Mrs Pointer having at the moment house-assistance from one of the lubras, Bony sat with Robin on the veranda overlooking the open space bordered by the men's quarters and outbuildings.

"How did the aborigines come in?" Bony asked, feeling lazy and greatly content. "Walked, I assume."

"Couldn't travel any other way, Bony. The girls and the old gins carried their belongings, the lordly masters strutting on ahead of them. I wish I were a man."

"I ignore your last remark. Did all the aborigines come in from Bore Ten?"

"All bar Tonto. He's lying up with a bad cold. Why the curiosity?"

"Have to gossip to keep your mind off asking me questions," Bony told her. "I've not forgotten your early threat."

"Don't let it worry you, Bony. I've a little more respect for you than I had. Dozens of detectives go tramping all over the place for nothing; in a few days you find Brandt's bicycle and the remains of the swags. What more did you find?"

"Lots. And lots I have still to find, and shall, now that the rain has washed the dust off them. What whisky does your father drink?"

"What . . . whisky? Father doesn't drink whisky. What an extraordinary question."

"I'm glad to hear it. Spirits are bad for any man. Is the telephone to the main homestead still in order?"

"It was this morning, when Dad was speaking to Mr Long. Go on. I'm liking this, Bony. Ask all your questions and beware of mine."

Robin's dark eyes were mischievous. She looked cool and not a little alluring, her black hair short, and the style suited the shape of her head. Were it not for the faint hint of superiority towards the male sex, Bony's romantic soul might have been warmed by the fire of her challenge. He said:

"One more question, and you may begin on me. Why did

you have your hair cut at the time Paul Dickson was found murdered?"

"Because it needed cutting, silly."

CHAPTER 18

Fire in Black Opal

BONY WAS given no opportunity to repeat the question, for Robin's mother appeared and at once began chatting about the changed world, and of the hope it held for everyone. The men returned from the camp, and then old John had to ring Midnight Long and talk rain, ground feed, sheep and prospects of buying when everyone sought to buy. The great news, however, was that the manager would instruct his agent to purchase on the Fort Deakin account six hundred ewes. They would probably arrive with the Fort Deakin sheep from agistment.

When the Downers departed for Lake Jane, Bony requested permission to use the telephone and was conducted to Pointer's office.

"Sit down, Jim, and let us talk. You have the time?"

"Of course. Go ahead," Pointer assented readily. "From what we have been told about finding the bike and swag things in a gilgie hole, there seems to be plenty to talk about."

"The day before the rain came the Downers brought letters from me to post on. I suppose they are still here?"

"No. It happened that a Government bore-inspector went through on his way down to Mindee, and he took the mail. He was to stay the night at Fort Deakin, so I can't say how soon after that night of storm he got down to Mindee."

"Then I'd like to contact Sergeant Mawby."

"Sure. Just ring. Have to raise Mr Long. He'll put you through to Mindee."

"Oh, it's you, Inspector," exclaimed Midnight across forty-five miles of waterlogged country. "Nice to hear your voice."

Bony inquired about his letters, and was told they had been taken to Mindee four days back. Long said he would raise Sergeant Mawby and ring back when he made the connection.

"You won't be busy until the sheep come home, will you?"

Bony asked Pointer, and the overseer said he could give all the time Bony desired. His dark eyes were always calm, always without barriers, and Bony now relied on his judgment of Jim Pointer.

"What we say here could be strictly in confidence, Jim?"

"Take it for granted."

"You ease my load." Bony lit a cigarette. "You heard from the Downers about the bike and swag remains. There are other matters I have kept to myself, and will continue to do so until there are further developments. I require information as well as assistance. Figuratively, I have reached a junction, and further investigation will take me along one road or the other. Please understand that I cannot see the end of the journey, and therefore asked for your assurance not to repeat our conversation. Now, tell me. Tonto was left at Bore Ten, allegedly with a bad cold. Did none of his relatives stay with him?"

"No. His wife and all came in with Nuggety Jack."

"They came in today?"

"Yesterday, late. I let them camp back of the woolshed, as their usual camping place here is under water."

"This Tonto fellow. Wasn't it he who was severely man-handled some considerable time ago?"

"The same," answered Pointer. "Any hospital would have taken him in, but he wouldn't leave. They're tough all right."

"And now he could be sick, or could be recovering from a thrashing I gave him, Jim. That day I found the bike and the remains of what is certainly two swags, I was followed. I was sure of it when the moon came up and Downer's heeler scented him. We arrived at the Rudder's gate after dark. I knew it made a row when opened. I made sure it did when I opened it, and again when I closed it. The trailer knew I had passed through.

"Then I waited for him. He didn't open the gate, but climbed over it. That heeler is well trained. Having been told to keep back, he kept away, and I proceeded to mark my trailer with a length of fencing wire. He could be Tonto."

"You couldn't identify him?"

"Not before I branded him. When he had left at full speed, I identified his tracks and with the aid of matches. Blackfeller, without doubt. I could have arrested him, but he wouldn't have talked. What I intended was to identify him by my marks later on. If it should be proved that he was Tonto, then what was Tonto about, and who put Tonto up to it, and why?"

"We could run out to Bore Ten tomorrow and look Tonto over."

"He wouldn't be there when we arrived. No. I have a more subtle plan. We could . . . Excuse me."

Bony lifted the telephone, and Midnight Long said he would switch over to Mindee.

"Day, Mawbee; Bonaparte here. Nice rain."

"Beaut. Should do a lot of good. How are you?" The sergeant's voice was, as always, deceptively lazy.

"Staying at L'Albert for a few days. No time, I suppose, to have the lab. report of those hair specimens?"

"No. Had to go to Sydney. Could be another three to five days. Rain has delayed road traffic, as you'll know."

"Contact me when you have it, please." Bony idly glanced at Pointer, and for a moment their eyes met. "Reference Number Four in my letter. Period September–October last year. Ascertain date he left Mindee for Broken Hill, and date he returned to Mindee. It's physically possible that he did not proceed to Broken Hill. Ask your HQ to check on him at all hotels and garages for his truck."

The sergeant's voice was not now tired.

"Right, Inspector, I have that."

"At the same time, Mawby, I want to know if Number Four bought jewellery in Broken Hill. If possible at this late date, I'd like to know if he bought petrol before leaving Mindee, in addition to the usual filling of the petrol tank. That's all for the present."

"I'll check," came the sergeant's voice, and he enumerated the instructions. "You getting warm?"

"Merely a slight glow. How's the wife?"

"Has been worse. Rain seems to have helped her."

Replacing the instrument, Bony began to roll a cigarette, keeping his gaze on the chore, and Pointer was silent, watching the long brown fingers, and his mind racing here and there and shunning cul-de-sacs. He found himself caught in the net of Bonaparte's blue eyes. He could not see the lips which framed the word:

"Well?"

"I couldn't avoid listening and putting two to five," Pointer said.

"I wanted you to be able to put two to five, and take one

away, Jim. Honestly I don't know where we are going from here. I have investigated stubborn murder cases which have given me the thrill of the hunter. Other cases have provided me with the academic interest of the scientist watching the progress of an experiment. And yet other cases have brought me great sadness. I am beginning to feel that this case will fall into the last category. I am wishing I could walk out on it, and the wish is vain because I cannot walk out. I have become a prisoner of circumstances, as you and yours have become, and the Downers, and, I am thinking, so have Nuggety Jack and his people. How near tonight, in your utility, could you take me to Bore Number Ten?"

"Be lucky to get you half way, the state the track's in after dark."

"If we left at sundown, you might be able to take me several miles before darkness made travelling really difficult. There and back is twenty miles. A long walk. Were the track in normal condition, I would not want you to take me right to Bore Ten. Will you try?"

"Yes, of course. Leaving in daylight, we could get within three or four miles of the Bore, perhaps farther, with luck."

"Good! We'll do that, and leave without mentioning anything of the trip. Thanks, Jim."

2

Tonto was a full-blood who had gone to school and could tell you where, for example, Estonia is, and thus was one up on hundreds of white men and women in the Australian cities who would flunk the question. Geography was his strong point, as with all his race; drawing maps on sand is the accomplishment of the infant, and memorizing the outlines of objects comes very early in life. On leaving school he could read well, and could write, even writing love letters to the maiden he married eventually, which she couldn't read.

Tonto was just the average young aborigine in this era, when much money is spent on their education – and barriers erected to prevent them benefiting from it.

He was of the Dingo Totem, and of late it did seem that the Dog was bringing him bad luck. Even his own dogs had deserted him the previous day, preferring to track his wife, who had departed with the others for L'Albert to collect the reward for making rain. He had performed his part in the early rain-making ceremonies, too, and would have continued had not orders been issued to undertake a certain assignment.

One full day following a long night of loneliness was now getting into Tonto's hair, of which he had plenty, long and wavy and jet black. Of slightly independent spirit, he was no rebel against the authority of his elders.

Now lean and hungry, he squatted over his small fire amid the pine trees at Bore Ten, his whirlie empty and cold at his back, and beyond the firelight the world hidden behind a black curtain. All about him were the spirits of a thousand generations of forebears, and all of them together were not as powerful as Napoleon Bonaparte; who blew air down his neck and said:

"Careful, Tonto. Don't move. Feel the gun?"

Tonto did not move. He did feel the round impress of the automatic against his skin covering a kidney. He began breathing hard, overpowered by the respect owed a man who could steal up behind him and blow down his neck.

"Now lean back slowly and lie on your back, with your legs straight." Tonto obeyed, seeing Bony standing as a giant with the firelight flickering on the metal in his right hand.

"Stay like that. Rest in peace." Bony, with his feet worked additional wood on to and about the small fire, and soon tall flames rose to push away the encircling wall of night. "You may sit up, but keep your legs straight."

Tonto sat up and glowered across the fire to the man now squatting on his heels. His mind worked fast on a problem of relative speed: muscular action versus projectile. Finding the solution quite simple, he remained passive, and explored another problem: the relationship of the unarmed citizen who has his rights, whatever that means, and an armed policeman having blazing blue eyes and ferocious mien. He himself wasn't particularly handsome. A whitish welt extending down his left cheek to the point of his jaw spoiled his looks.

"The day before Nuggety Jack and Dusty made the rain, you followed me all around Rudder's," Bony accused. "You put up two kangaroos to prove it. You let a crow see you, and the crow proved it. You let the new wind come from you to my dog, and he proved it. You climbed over the gate at Rudder's and then I proved it, and branded you. Tonto, I don't like you."

In modern phraseology, silently Tonto asked: "So what?"

"You know that I am a top-feller policeman," Bony proceeded, hoping for one tiny grain of information. "You know why I came to L'Albert and why I went over to Lake Jane. I know that you followed me around Rudder's Paddock, and that you climbed the gate so that I wouldn't hear you following me, and I know that the brand on your face was done with a length of fence wire so that I would recognize you when I wanted to. We know much about each other, Tonto."

To sit on the ground with the legs straight and flat quickly becomes acutely uncomfortable for an aborigine accustomed to sitting on his heels, and so Bony granted permission for Tonto to raise his knees and clasp his hands in front of them. Knowing that to put questions direct to an aborigine in a hostile mood is to waste time and achieve no result, Bony continued to make statements, and hoped to gain information through reactions.

"I didn't mind you trailing me in Rudder's Paddock. In fact, you could have come with me, and we could have had a bitch about the drought and all that. I didn't mark you for following me that day. I marked you because I wanted to know who it was that let those dogs at Lake Jane stay chained up, so that they died."

The firelight glinted whitely at the corners of Tonto's eyes.

"That was a nasty thing to do, leaving those dogs to die of thirst when you were told to go to Lake Jane and loose them. I don't blame Nuggety Jack and the others belting into you for that. How would you like someone tying up your dogs till they perished of thirst?"

"Wouldn't mind," replied Tonto to this indirect question. "My flaming dogs cleared out and left me. Went after the missus and the kids."

"Perhaps you don't mind just now, Tonto. But those Lake Jane dogs didn't clear out and leave you. They didn't do anything to you. All you had to do was to let 'em loose."

Again the betraying flicker of white in the eyes, and Bony was satisfied that he had won a point. He ventured a direct question.

"Well, why didn't you let 'em loose?"

"I got sick. I got sick in the guts. I give it away."

"Well, in that case, Tonto, I'm sorry I marked you. Wouldn't have done if I'd known you took sick." Tonto brightened in the warmth of this expression of sympathy. "Suppose you knew why you were told to loose them."

"Didn't."

"But you were belted around for not doing what you were told."

No reply, merely the glint of firelight in the corners of Tonto's eyes.

"Why belt you around?" pressed Bony hopefully. "The dogs are dead, anyway. And what's a few dogs after all? They didn't belong to Nuggety Jack, or Dusty or any other black-feller. Are you sure you were belted around for not loosing the dogs? Were you belted around for something else?"

Tonto went on strike, but he should have closed his eyes. He was beginning to understand that he had fallen into a trap, and his eyes gave him away.

"Pretty soon Nuggety Jack is going to see my tracks here, and know you and I had a little talk," Bony pointed out. "What say you go on walkabout for a week? Tell you what, Tonto. You go on down to Mindee and see Sergeant Mawby. I'll tele-phone to the sergeant and tell him to give you a job at the Police Station, cleaning up and that sort of work. He might make you his tracker. I know his regular tracker cleared off down to the Murray. What do you think of that?"

"No ruddy good. The sergeant he lock me up."

"But he won't when I tell him to give you a job."

Tonto was melting from the fire of rising anger. And anger cutteth a man off at the knees.

"All right, then. What are you going to do? Sit here and wait for Nuggety and the boys to bash you for talking to me, for telling me you went sick instead of loosing the dogs?"

"To hell with you. You got me into this. You . . ."

"Who told you to follow me around Rudder's?"

"Nug . . . I'm not saying. To hell with you."

"Well, you'll carry the bag," Bony unnecessarily pointed out. "You stay here and be half-murdered by the boys, or you clear off down to Mindee and have the sergeant keep you from being half-murdered, or you go off on walkabout, any-where you like. I'll tell you something, Tonto. If I see you in L'Albert, I'll have you in jail for ten years for not letting those dogs go." Bony held up with his left hand two plugs of tobacco. "I'm leaving these here for you. When I'm gone, grab 'em and go for your life."

CHAPTER 19

The Duel

IT WAS ten o'clock when Pointer and Bony returned to L'Albert from what Bony felt had been a profitable trip. Knowing his country, the overseer had been able to reach a spot within two miles of Bore Ten before it became dark, and the return journey had been comparatively easy by following the tracks made during daylight.

Instead of informing Pointer what had transpired at Tonto's campfire, Bony took him further into his confidence relative to the tracks made by the car or utility in Rudder's Paddock, and which had been responsible for leading him and the dog to the gilgie hole.

In view of Tonto's admissions which brought Nuggety Jack into this still shrouded picture, Bony wanted to know whether the aborigine had petrol at the time Paul Dickson had been killed. Pointer was positive that Nuggety Jack had no petrol, and that his car was then being drawn by a couple of horses, while Bony was sure that the car the tracks of which he had followed had been jacked to get started, and was, therefore, petrol-driven.

On returning to the homestead, Bony had asked permission to use the office, in which to write reports and meditate. He had gone direct to the office, and now was seated before the large-scale wall map, and sideways to the table desk.

On this map of the northern portion of Fort Deakin, called L'Albert, with Lake Jane to the east and Jorkin's Soak to the west, was noted all the bores and wells and connecting roads or tracks, as well as ranges of sandhills, water courses, and depressions having collected water during the last hundred years. Someone, probably a previous investigator, had written in pencil the name of everyone living within this area at the time Paul Dickson was found dead at Lake Jane.

Bony had read in the Official Summary several theories covering these two murders separated by eighteen miles of near desert, and he had listened to further theories given by the Downers, and the Pointers, and all of them he discarded because there was no basis of fact on which they were built.

His own investigation had been advanced to the point that the two murders had been an inside job, meaning that they had been committed by some person or persons within the area covered by that wallmap.

No police investigator, no local person, had put forward a plausible motive for killing first Dickson, and then Brandt. Even now, at this stage of his investigation, Bony could not presume a motive having any degree of plausibility. However, he felt justified in seriously considering the theory that both murders had taken place at the same place and time, and that the body of Brandt had been conveyed eighteen miles to another place for burial in order to (a) lead the police to believe that Dickson had been murdered by Brandt, and (b) direct police activity to hunting down Brandt and prevent police focusing attention on this locality and those who lived here. Had not Brandt's body been found, the police would have hunted for him until writing off their investigation altogether.

Now, owing to the behaviour of an aborigine named Tonto, plus Tonto's disclosures, he, Bonaparte, could focus his attention upon Nuggety Jack, and his Medicine Man, Dusty.

Bony swung himself to sit square to the desk, and he rolled six cigarettes before lighting one and drawing to him Pointer's work diary for the previous year. The first date which held him was August 1st, and read: 'Nuggety Jack came in with dog scalps and was credited with £26. He asked for petrol and it was refused on the score that the fuel supply was low.' In parenthesis, Pointer had written: 'Jack is doing all right at Bore Ten. Persuaded him to leave fifteen pounds of the dog money in credit as the future is going to be hard for him as for everyone else.'

The account of the visit by the police to investigate the death at Lake Jane occupied so much space that a blank page had been gummed into the book, and another entry told of the visit to Lake Jane by the writer and his wife and daughter to see the water flowing over the Crossing and into the lake's dry bed. And in brackets: 'First time the women had ever seen water running into Lake Jane. We all went paddling on the Crossing. And met in the centre the two Downers who paddled back with us to our side where the billy was boiled. Quite a happy little picnic.'

Another entry read: 'Mr Long asked to be driven out to see

Eric Downer and their sheep. Took five 40-gal. drums of petrol and engine oil, in case needed by the Downers. Called at their homestead, and proceeded to Rudder's Well. Country out there looks plain terrible. Found Eric D. camped about three miles from Well, and cutting scrub for about 500 sheep where he's carting water for them, to save walking. Left the petrol and oil with him. He might pull the sheep through. If it rains.'

Weeks afterwards Pointer had written: 'Robin ran over to the Downers. She reported that Eric D. had killed the last hundred of their sheep for the wool and hides. Later, on phone, Mr Long agreed it had been a great battle. Told him Robin says she read somewhere that a battle is never won until a battle is lost.'

"How true," murmured Bony. "How many battles did I lose before I won one." He was deep in meditation when there was a knock on the door, and Robin asked if she might come in. Bony opened it, and she entered carrying a supper tray.

"As you are too busy to have supper with us, I've come to have supper with you. May I?"

"Assuredly," assented Bony, and hastily pushed aside the open diary to make place for the tray. "We'll sup in harmony, and fire questions at each other like bullets in a battle."

Each sat sideways to the desk, and the light from the oil lamp fell upon her sleek black hair, and showed her oval face to advantage. She wore a white sheath dress which also enhanced her figure. In this light the golden flecks in her eyes were pronounced. She looked at Bony quizzingly, taking careful stock of him, from his hair, so like her own, to his long fingers. The moment held a spell, which she broke by leaning forward and reading the entry in the diary he had last read. The vivacity departed, and sadly she said:

"That was a terrible thing, Bony. I think of it often: killing the last of those sheep; and all that Eric went through and saw and heard before."

"That was the battle he lost. What was the battle he won?"

"He hasn't won the battle yet, Bony. That's still to come."

He watched as she poured coffee into the china cups, then said:

"Might I be frank? Do you think we could be friends enough to be frank with each other?"

He found those dark eyes had the power of probing equal to

his own, but he met them as though engaged in a duel, and awaited her answer expectantly.

"I don't know," she replied. "You see, I don't know you. To me you are an entirely new experience. You remind me sometimes of a man who worked here called Harry Thrumb." Their eyes continued the duel. "His father was white and his mother was black. He was better-looking than you, and he had what we used to call 'sex-appeal'. But he was superficial. No higher than many of the school-taught aborigines. You're not in his class, Bony. You're not in any class I've ever come in contact with. So I don't know about being frank. Not now, if ever."

An impish smile was born on his dark face, and without severing the eye-lock, he said:

"Well, do you like your coffee cold?"

That broke it, and she managed a soft laugh, saying:

"You see what I mean? You're not in any class I've met before."

"Then let us fence. You won't object to that, I'm sure. We should both be good at it."

"I'm not too confident."

"I shall be the first to cry for mercy. Sugar? I suppose you miss your horses these days?"

"I do, but it won't be long before we have the horses home. The herbage is springing fast."

"And soon the drought will be merely an unpleasant memory."

"It will ever be a nightmare to me. Something I shall always remember and shudder at."

"Why, then, keep those pictures of it to remind you?"

"I may not keep them, or some of them. They represent more than the agony of animals."

"The battle that Eric lost was the same battle you lost?"

"What do you mean? I didn't battle to save sheep."

"Not sheep. Something else associated with the battle to save sheep. What has come between you and Eric?"

The vivid face fractionally darkened, and her eyes hardened. Without looking at him, she said:

"Don't you think you are being too venturesome?"

"Yes and no. Just now you told me I am outside your experience. You are within mine. I am older than you by many years. You are fighting a battle following a battle. So is Eric.

Both of you lost one battle and only you hope to win this one. Perhaps Eric doesn't realize he's also fighting this battle, the one you are engaged in, but he will. It is because I don't like the odds that I am a little perturbed. They say that the formula for making successful films is quite simple: 'Girl finds boy. Girl loses boy. Girl gets boy.' You found Eric. Then you lost him. Now you have to get him back. To make a happy film, Robin."

"I don't see that it can possibly concern you, Bony. But you are right. Something did come between Eric and me, and that was the drought. Shall we talk of something else?"

"No."

"Your pardon!"

"You heard me. I said 'No' because it wasn't the drought which came between you and Eric, but something during the drought." Robin attempted to stand, but his hand restrained the action. "Don't go, please. Let's talk it out."

It was the new quiet voice of authority which now kept her seated, for here was a man she had not seen before. The easygoing, faintly teasing, politely pleasant Bony was no more. No longer was there about him the air of one conscious of being one degree lower in the social scale because of the accident of birth. Robin tried to remind herself that after all he was a half-caste, like Thrumb, like the others. Then she realized she was being silly, and alarm flowed into her mind, as it must into the mind of the rabbit at the instant the jaws of the trap snap upon its foot.

"I would, indeed, be crudely impertinent to probe into your personal problem were I not gravely perturbed by the feeling that it is associated in some way with the larger problem on which I am engaged," he said. "Even so, I would not speak of it to you were I not beginning to fear that other hearts than yours might be broken."

"What do you mean?" she heard herself ask.

"All of us have that sixth sense commonly called intuition," he went on. "Women have it stronger than men, and aborigines have it stronger than white women. I have it, that sixth sense which warns of a danger to come, which is a premonition of approaching disaster. Intuition isn't knowledge, and I am unable, therefore, to tell you in words what it is I fear. I can say, and shall say now, that you are not withholding from me, a policeman, information of concern to my investigation, but you are withholding what amounts to a suspicion of something which might be of value to me."

A stillness had settled about Robin Pointer, and her eyes were void of expression, as though determinedly refusing him access to her thoughts.

"I admit to one weakness, at least," Bony said, and now he was less stern. "Quite often it creates for me a disadvantage. I am too easily influenced by sentiment. You have been nice to me, and so I am unable to probe, to test, to cross-examine you merely because the subject might be of assistance in my official investigation. You don't disarm me, because I was never armed. To use a common term, I am passing the buck to you."

"There is nothing for me to tell you," Robin said, figuratively shaking herself. "I may have a suspicion, and I'm not even sure that I have. It is all so vague that – well, I couldn't put it into words. Do you suspect me of something? Why did you ask why I had had my hair cut at the time of the murders?"

"At the time of Dickson's murder," he corrected. "You have an admirer in Constable Sefton, and he mentioned to me how much the new style suits you. You will recall that at the time I asked the question we were fencing. When fencing, all is fair, don't you agree?"

"I don't think I do." Robin gazed searchingly at him. "I don't think I shall ever want to fence with you again. D'you think that my heart is broken?"

"No. Only that it could be. It will depend, perhaps, very greatly on yourself. For illustration. This office is now full of cigarette smoke. It depends on yourself whether you open the door to fresh air or continue to be slightly uncomfortable. The past drought is not unlike the air of this office, but the door is opened by the rain, and all the world is again fresh and lovely. Now you could paint a picture of sand dunes covered with green grass and herbage and massed with flowers. Why did you paint that one you titled 'Never the Twain shall Meet'?"

"Because the East *is* the East, and the West *is* the West; the black and the white. And never can they meet deeply, spiritually."

"Kipling could have been wrong. The qualifying abverb is the error. It should have been 'seldom', not 'never'."

"No!" she exclaimed. "I won't accept that. It is never, never, never." Standing she took up the supper tray. Tears were in her eyes, and anger in her voice. "I didn't want to fence. You made me. Goodnight."

Bony opened the door for her, and when again he was seated he told himself:

"The odds weren't even. I wasn't fair."

CHAPTER 20

A Virgin!

FOLLOWING many months of having to use hard well-water for household laundry, the coming of the rain to fill the house tanks was indeed a blessing.

At seven the next morning, Mrs Pointer and Robin were planning to give the aboriginal washerwomen a full day, being careful to keep from them fragile articles, so easily damaged by energetic zeal.

The workers arrived at seven-thirty. There was Mrs Nuggety Jack, elderly, small and bossy. There was Hattie, the wife of the Medicine Man and Chief Rain-maker, a woman of vast proportions, talkative, and a constant giggler. They were accompanied by two boys who were to chop wood for the coppers, to keep the water boiling that so much steam would be raised as almost to asphyxiate any human being in the laundry. These people invariably underdo it or overdo it. By 8 am the works were in full production.

At a safe distance, ie, from the wood heap, Bony watched the steam pouring from the laundry door and windows, and with him were the two boys assigned to feed the coppers. At first they were suspicious of him; when this vanished, they were as full of questions as a hive is of bees. Firstly they wanted to know where he was born. Secondly they wished to know what inspector's rank meant, and finally they skirted about the subject of the murders, and wanted to hear what he had found out about them, and who he was going to arrest. Neither was unsophisticated, Robin having taught them the three R's, and Nuggety Jack having a battery radio set.

Now and then one of the washerwomen would emerge from the steam and shriek for more wood. Eventually there was trundled from the laundry a wheelbarrow loaded with washed clothes, the vehicle being pushed by the fat lubra, and escorted by Mrs Nuggety, who directed the way to the many clothes-lines. Much argument ensued, Mrs Nuggety being a born organizer who insisted that sheets occupy one line, the blankets another, with a third given to the unmentionables, while the Medicine Man's wife was obviously inclined to be casual enough to drape the washing over the wood heap.

Bony felt his day was well begun, and that his present occupation was preferable to tramping about at Rudder's Well. The two boys, aged about fourteen, wore only drill shorts. The women wore coloured kerchiefs over their black hair; their skirts were hitched above their knees; their cotton blouses flapped open at the neck and the sleeves were rolled as high as possible. Eyes were bright and coal black. Teeth were large and white, the chocolate skin was bedewed with perspiration. Nothing is so elevating as the feeling of being important.

The women had to pass Bony on their way to the clothesline, and when they were about to pass again with the empty wheel-barrow, Bony was standing, and greeted them with a comradely smile. The fat one smiled in return and giggled Mrs Nuggety frowned, then was intrigued.

"How's work going today?" he asked, and they halted when the first natural shyness had been conquered.

"Good-oh! How you doing these days?" replied the little woman, whose eyes were examining Bony feature by feature, and then his arms, torso, and legs. "Pretty good rain, eh?"

"Good black-feller rain," agreed Bony, returning the careful scrutiny. The other woman, who had been bending over the barrow handles, stood up and giggled. She said:

"Plenty tobacco, plenty rain. By and by more rain, more tobacco."

She, too, was scrutinized from head to foot. No one was embarrassed. The women were captivated by the colour of the stranger's eyes.

They moved on to the laundry, and Bony sat again on a log, and smoked.

These people, he knew, were advancedly assimilated, for complete assimilation isn't achieved by the aborigine via swift passage from one State to another, as the foreign national is granted citizen rights at a Town Hall ceremony. Assimilation is gradual, and requires several generations to produce the Mr and Mrs Smiths and Browns who live in city suburbs.

The people now occupying Bonaparte's attention were two generations towards assimilation. They were still inhibited by their traditions, and still, at least partially, influenced by their origins. Proof lay in the absence of a front tooth in each woman, knocked out when sealed into their tribe. Proof also was to be seen in two short cicatrices like chevrons between their breasts, denoting they belonged to a man. At this time they interested Bony in determining the degree of assimilation by the white race.

Robin Pointer came from the side veranda wheeling an old pram loaded with articles to wash, actually, house curtains, and, parking the load at the laundry doorway, she came and sat with Bony, and asked for a cigarette.

"I've earned it, Bony. Do make one."

With unusual care, he rolled a cigarette, tamped the ends with a match, and offered it to her to lick the paper. Having struck the match, he was regarded above the flame by studiously dark eyes, and she said:

"Day off? Holiday?"

"I shall begin work presently, when you are free."

"What have I to do with whether you work or not?"

"It often happens that a man has to be prodded to work by a woman," Bony declared. "Besides, I have been working. I've been overseeing those two boys cutting and carting fuel for the laundry. Quite exhausting."

"It would be," Robin mocked. "Poor hard-working man! Never mind, though. It's gone half past nine, and morning tea is ready. Would you like to accompany me thither?"

"Them is encouraging words, lady. And then yon."

"Yon?"

"Thither to the morning tea and yon to inspect the homestead under your guidance."

"Ah! More mischief, Bony. Well, to be forewarned is to be armed. Full of clichés this morning, aren't we?"

"As the boys are full of questions."

An hour later they set off on the 'inspection', and Robin wanted to show him the motor shed, but he suggested the shearing shed, as he knew all about motor sheds. Then at the shearing shed he confessed that he was boringly familar with shearing sheds, and suggested visiting the aborigines in their temporary camp.

About the shearing shed human traffic had been light, and

where the wind had piled sand against the walls and the posts of the drafting yards the grass was already six inches high, and the plants of buckbush and wild spinach were beginning to mass. In the sugar gums the cicadas shrilled ceaselessly their love calls. They ought to have left their hibernating ground holes in the spring. Now it was autumn.

"Why do you want to visit the aborigines?" Robin asked, and could not prevent the betrayal of strain.

"All tourists want to talk with the aborigines," countered Bony. "For me they are of special interest, anthropological interest. We shall gather them about us, and you can tell me if one lamb is missing from the fold."

The aborigines were camped in a small grove of uniformly shaped cabbage trees, providing shade and a perfect setting for those who sat or lounged under them. The children playing in the sun would normally have raced to the protection of the trees at sight of the visitors, but, recognizing Robin, they ran to meet them.

Escorted by the children, who, singularly enough, were either naked or dressed in flimsy finery, Robin and Bony approached the camp until met by Nuggety Jack and Dusty and several other men.

"We were out on a little walkabout," Robin explained, "and Inspector Bonaparte said he would like to visit you all."

All eyes were directed to Bony, serious eyes in happy faces. One naked toddler clutched Robin's hand, and another, not to be outdone, shyly touched Bony's hand and became immensely proud when his grubby fingers were held.

"Been a wonderful rain," he remarked to the men. "Mr Long says that as you did such a great job making the rain, Mr Pointer is to hand out another case of jam, and another box of tobacco.

They grinned appreciation, and Nuggety thought to strike the iron when hot. He said:

"Getting pretty low in sugar. Any chance of a bit?"

"We can tell Mr Long that Mr Pointer added a twenty-pound bag."

Nuggety, delighted by his victory, asked:

"The old woman doing her stuff in the laundry, Miss Robin?"

"She and Mrs Dusty were working hard when we left," replied Robin. "Why, Larry, what did you do to your face?"

"I fell over and hit it with a stick, Miss Robin," replied the little boy, whose cheek and forehead were badly cut and bruised.

"Let me see." Robin knelt to examine the nasty wound, and the other children crowded about her. "You must come to the house and have it bathed properly, Larry."

The women and girls now had joined the group of men, and some of them evidently had hastily slipped on their best dresses before appearing. Bony noticed two girls of the same age and slim build wearing dresses of identical colour and style. Observing his interest, they smiled, and whispered to each other, and revealed a missing tooth in each mouth. An old woman laughed at something said by another, and she, too, had a tooth missing. A young woman, who was wearing only a skirt, took a baby from another woman and proceeded to suckle it. All the women and the older girls bore between their breasts the chevron cicatrice of marriage, or promise in marriage.

Robin's popularity with these people was plainly evident. The smaller children clustered about her, and the girls asked questions, one even asking if she had other picture magazines 'with new dresses in them'. The men wanted to hear about Bony's origin: Where did he come from? Had he been a policeman all his life? Was he married, and how many children did he have? Their chests and arms bore the cicatrices of orthodox initiation.

Hitherto unaware of her presence, Bony saw the young woman Pointer had called Lottee, whom Mrs Long wanted at the homestead for another spell of domestic work. She was now with the elderly women standing behind their men.

"Oh, by the way, Lottee," he said, beckoning slightly with his head. "Mrs Long again asked if you would like to go to the river and housemaid for her."

The men parted to permit the girl to stand nearer, and Lottee shook her head. The space between her and Bony was bridged by their eyes, and Bony felt the personality behind her fearless gaze.

"Like I told Mr Pointer, I don't want to go to the river," she said, her voice low, the words distinct and without accent.

"Don't want to leave the old man, you see, Inspector," said Nuggety Jack, and everyone laughed, including Lottee.

The girl did not have a front tooth missing. She did not

bear the mark of a man's woman on her chest, for although she was pleasingly clad in a bright blue dress, the low neckline permitted Bony to glimpse that much.

How old? These girls mature early. Perhaps eighteen. At first sight that might be a reasonable guess. For an aborigine, she was good-looking, and the more one did look at her, the more one noted the refinement of features and the entire absence of any trace of mixed ancestry. Bony was strongly reminded of Marie, his wife, when, as youth and maid, they had been married and ran away together to the haven they made.

This girl wasn't a half-caste as was Marie, but she had Marie's brown eyes, which were such wonderful windows to Marie's calm spirit that later stresses had never ruffled. This girl was now regarding Bony without bashfulness or coquetry, regarding him curiously, judging him; and deep in his mind was the image of his wife when they were young, and not so young.

"Very well, I'll tell Mr Long you don't want to go," he said casually, and bent to the tot still clinging to his hand. He recalled other Lottees who had this same elusive quality, so difficult to pinpoint. Because they were rare, they persisted in memory. It was not feminine magnetism, although this was present, but rather an aloofness of spirit which nothing mundane could influence.

As he stood up, his gaze rose from her shapely ankles, re-markable in an aborigine, to her shapely body, and to her neck, from which was suspended a red cord attached to the inevitable dilly-bag concealed by her dress. For a moment, only he and she existed. In that moment their eyes met, and hers did not waver.

"I admire your bracelet," he said easily. "A charm bracelet! Pity you lost one of the horses. Have you had it long?"

"Long time now," interposed Nuggety Jack, and Dusty supported him. "I give it to her when she come seventeen," and again the Medicine Man backed him.

"Let me see, please," Bony requested, offering an inviting hand. He slipped the bracelet from her wrist. Fine silver chains held a tiny black horse and a tiny brown one. There was no horse attached to the third chain. His eyes challenged her, but, like his wife, she had the power to defeat his intention with calm and steady appraisal.

"You know, Lottee, you can be lucky," he said lightly, and the men about them laughed. He held out his other hand, palm upward, and on the palm the white horse.

"I must be," she agreed, and for the second time smiled into his eyes. "Where did you find it?"

"On the kitchen woodheap. I was talking to the boys this morning, and saw it between two old blocks. As I told you, you can be lucky."

"Thank you, Inspector. That's where I must have lost it."

When he turned away he couldn't decide if there was alarm or mockery in her voice.

CHAPTER 21

They who Question

"THAT neighbourly call just now roused my curiosity," Robin said, when passing the store, fronted by a long bench. She suggested they sit there, and that he make two cigarettes. "What do you think of our Lottee?"

"A fine-looking girl for an aborigine. How old would she be?"

"Twenty-four last January."

"And how old are you?"

"How . . . How old am I? Now, look you here, Mister Inspector Napoleon Bonaparte, it was my curiosity which was roused, not yours."

"No matter. I can ask your father." Having made the cigarettes he struck a match, handed her a cigarette and said deliberately: "Those that ask questions should be prepared to answer others. I think Lottee is rather unusual. You do, too, I take it."

"Very," agreed Robin, adding as an afterthought, "for an aborigine."

"I saw that she isn't married or promised in marriage. I noticed, too, that she hasn't a front tooth knocked out like the other women. How old did you say you are?"

"Twenty. . . . Stop it, Bony. Does your wife ever want to shake you till your teeth drop out?"

"Only in play," he replied. "At the moment you and I are

not playing. I asked you how old you are, when I know the answer, because my mind was off at a tangent, and didn't want to bother returning. You are two years older than Lottee. You are gifted and educated, and she can read and write. And yet, Robin, compared with her you are naïve. Don't take offence at that. I, too, have not her depth."

The girl examined her cigarette, and gazed pensively towards the main house. Presently Bony said:

"So many people fail to see these aborigines for what they are. To regard them as uncouth savages is such a boost for the ego, and yet, search as you might, you won't find a moron among them. I know an aboriginal head man who might have skipped five thousand years to come down to this age, for mankind has deteriorated mentally and spiritually. Lottee gave me the same impression as that head man did."

"I don't like her," Robin said, and Bony told her he was aware of it. "I mean," amended Robin, "I mean, I don't dislike her for the impression you received. She has a kind of feline power all about her, and within, which is too much for my ego. She makes me feel ignorant and small, and I resent it. After all she is only an aborigine. Now tell me truly, what does she do to you?"

"She is most tactful. She doesn't speak of temptation."

Abruptly Robin turned to him and gripped his hand.

"Stop fencing. Where did you find that horse?"

"Is that important?"

"Very. Tell me."

"You tell me why it is so important for you to know."

"It's not that important." Robin stood. "We'd better go to the house. Lunch will be called any minute. We're always at loggerheads; anyway, I think you are beginning to bore me."

Standing with her, Bony laughed openly and delightedly, and colour mounted to her face, and anger blazed. "I wish you were a little boy, and not as old as my father, my grand-father actually."

"There could come a time when to lean on an ancient reed is better than to lean upon the wind." Now serious once more he added: "We'll talk again sometime before the explosion. I have a premonition of an impending explosion."

"Perhaps, afterwards, we won't be always quarrelling, Bony."

"Perhaps, afterwards, we may be in tiny pieces."

Jim Pointer appeared on the veranda to call Bony to the office telephone, and when Bony begged to be excused, Robin's eyes were wistful.

Closing the door, he picked up the receiver to hear Mawby say:

"Reference Number Four, Inspector. No trace of him in Broken Hill between the dates in question. As requested, I sent Sefton north as far as Soak. He has just returned, wasn't once bogged. The Jorkins say they hadn't seen Number Four at their place for at least three years. Sefton inquired about the truck, and one of the Jorkins remembered he'd noticed a truck track two miles this side of their place. Truck driven off the road and proceeded across country in a north-easterly direction. Young feller thought at the time the driver was on business which was no concern of the Jorkins clan. The imprints of the tyres, according to young Jorkin, were of the same make that Number Four is known to have."

"Puzzle pieces falling into place," Bony said without enthusiasm. "Your information was needed. Please try tracing purchase of additional petrol."

"I've done that," Mawby stated in his official manner. "Number Four bought two 40-gallon drums of petrol and a case of eight gallons of engine oil, for which he paid cash. In addition to a filled petrol tank on the morning he left Mindee."

"Anything else, Mawby?"

"Odds and ends. The gent must have prepared for quite a trip. Also paid cash for a quantity of foodstuffs and a chain wire-strainer, plus a five-pound box of plug tobacco. Now what would he want with a wire-strainer?"

"You tell me," suggested Bony, and Mawby laughed. "Your reports help a lot, and it's possible I shall ask you to run out and lend a hand in a few days or a week. I'll be in a hurry when I do call."

"I'll be ready and waiting, Inspector. I take it you're running true to form."

"You may, Mawby. *Au revoir!*"

Bony sought for Pointer and found him reading a journal on the veranda.

"What you and I need, Jim, is a short holiday," he began. "Three or four days, perhaps. You know, duck-shooting and the like. We'd want camp gear and tucker, of course, Could you manage it?"

Without hesitation, the overseer accepted the ball, and Bony accompanied him to collect shotguns, ammunition and camping equipment.

2

Following much showy preparation they drove off on the track to the main homestead, and having proceeded three miles, Pointer was asked to stop the utility, and Bony explained that his objective was as far west even as Jorkin's Soak, with shooting game as a sideline.

"I think it unwise to let anyone know what we're up to," continued Bony. "From this point, could you make a very wide detour to miss the homestead and reach the road to Blazer's beyond it?"

"Yes. But if you want to go over to Jorkin's Soak we could cross country from here and have no need to go via Blazer's."

"Better still, Jim. We won't want for water, that's sure."

Water! Water lay everywhere; in pools both great and small; in depressions and ancient sand channels. Fading in memory was that dusty-grey-brown half-dead dehydrated land; a nightmare vision of a strange hell; for here and now was the real world of sparkling waters, and the soft breeze waving the vivid green of grass and herbage. Of animal life there was nothing as yet, and the birds had still to come.

Pointer had of necessity to detour, to miss sandhills and avoid soft ground. Once they were bogged and lost half an hour. Neither man spoke much, both busy with his own thoughts, Bony of that man who drove his truck off the road near Jorkin's Soak, and Pointer wondering what this present trip was all about.

"Almost certain that this creek will stop us," Pointer predicted. They came to a line of box skirting the creek, and, as the overseer guessed, the creek was running high and fast. "Walton's Hole is on the other side and lower down. Nothing there but a well and drafting yards belonging to Ballara."

"Anyone coming from Jorkin's Soak would cross the creek at this point?" pressed Bony.

"That's so."

"It's about half an hour to sundown. We'll camp here for the night. If you'll make camp, I'll prospect on foot."

Choosing hard and dry ground, Pointer made a fire and dragged near to it much dead wood to serve till the morning. He watched Bony going up the creek, noted how he walked on the balls of his feet, and his head held as though low on his shoulders. The stretchers were set up beside the utility, and the tucker box and cooked provisions placed ready for dinner.

It was dusk when Bony returned. He pointed upward, and the overseer witnessed two wide wedges of duck passing high, two black chevrons, the mark of possession, against the cool greening sky.

Later they sat on their heels before the fire and smoked, and presently Bony proceeded to allay Pointer's long-pent curiosity.

"I'm beginning to think, Jim, that you are as naturally patient as I am. You ask no questions. You are the perfect travelling companion. I will tell you a little.

"In general it has been thought that the murderer of Carl Brandt and Paul Dickson came down from the north to Lake Jane. Although I am gravely doubtful, that might well be so. But, at that time, a man drove a truck from the south, then crossed the creek here and proceeded in that direction."

Bony pointed slightly north of where the sun had set. He said:

"What lies in that direction?"

"A disused bore called Number Eleven."

"Ah! I remember it on the map. On the same line as Bore Ten, Blazer's Dam, and this Bore Eleven. Possible to raise water?"

"Windlass and bucket. Water's brackish, and I wouldn't like having to live on it. You didn't find the tracks of that truck seven months after they were made and after ten inches of rain, did you?"

"Yes. I tracked him going and tracked him coming back this way."

From looking at the dark face illumined by the fire, Pointer stared into the lazily leaping flames. Abruptly he asked:

"What the hell would the feller drive to Bore Eleven for? There's nothing there. There's nothing beyond it. Seems silly, but are you confident about the age of the tracks?"

Bony nodded, rolled a cigarette and lit it with a fired stick about two yards long. Under other circumstances, Jim Pointer would have been amused. Now he waited tensely for further enlightenment, a big man sitting on his heels with the ease of long practice, his large square face lacking even the hint of his daughter's vivacity. To him time dragged before Bony spoke again.

"I am not liking my job, Jim. You know, chasing a criminal is similar to going on a journey. One gains the impression of travelling from place to place, and not knowing where the place ahead will be. Now and then the traveller can see ahead what the weather is going to be: clear, stormy, foggy. And there is no going back. I am facing foggy weather, and I never liked fog."

A few minutes later Bony decided on bed, and for some time thereafter the overseer lay looking up at the stars and wondering what kind of a road he himself was on.

The next morning the wind came early and hot from the north, promising to reduce the risk of bogging with every hour.

To confirm his discovery of the previous evening, as well as to provide interest for Pointer to balance information withheld, Bony directed his driver to the area on which the tracks of the truck had been preserved. However, no matter from which angle Pointer studied the ground, he could see no marks, and frankly admitted defeat.

"They are there, all right," Bony assured him. "I'll put a foot in one of the wheel tracks." Pointer ruefully abandoned further effort, and Bony asked:

"Assuming that he proceeded in that direction, he would reach Bore Eleven?"

"Yes. He'd reach the L'Albert boundary about three miles from here. Bore Number Eleven is five miles beyond the gate."

"Then we'll proceed direct to the gate. I'll stand up at the back. I might be fortunate enough to sight his tracks again."

Standing at the rear of the cabin, when his eyes were twenty inches higher than its roof, Bony could see much farther and without interruption. The country was similar to that crossed the previous day. He sighted no tracks on this cross-country section. He saw only two blue cranes looking into a pool of water which he was sure was merely two inches deep.

Presently he could see the fence ahead, and silently complimented the driver on aiming his utility directly to it. Arrived at the gate, both jumped to the ground.

"Damn it, Bony! I shouldn't have doubted, but I did," confessed Pointer. "There's his tracks, I'll bet a million. Excepting Nuggety Jack no one's been out here for a couple of years.

That's the track of a truck dead in the gateway. Even the rain didn't wash it out, as you can see. Do you know the feller who was driving the truck all that time ago?"

"Yes," was the answer, and Pointer wondered at the sadness of the voice.

CHAPTER 22

The Civil Servant

DIFFICULT country demanded an hour of time to reach Number Eleven Bore. Here the hut was in bad repair, and the stockyards would need attention before again being used. Once there had been a windmill to raise water; now there was a windlass with a bucket attached to wire rope, and the bucket was useless. In its place was a much rusted petrol tin.

They had seen no tracks of the truck since passing through the boundary gate, and Bony said, brows slightly raised:

"Why, do you think, was that truck driven into this paddock?"

"Ask me another, Bony. I don't know and can't guess."

"We'll prospect out wide," Bony decided. "I'll stand at the back to get a higher sighting-elevation. We know he came into this paddock, and he must have had a purpose."

"You reckon he's important?"

"Yes, Jim, very important."

Pointer drove from the Bore for a full half-mile, when he began the circle which had the Bore as its centre, and which, when completed, would cut across the tracks of anyone visiting the Bore, were they washed out or not. He had proceeded on this giant circle for three-quarters of the way, when Bony stamped the order to stop. There was a short line of horse droppings left when the horse was passing between the Bore and a wood or copse of Australian black oak. The trees occupied a low ridge, and Pointer was asked to drive to them.

"If I had to camp at the Bore for a few days, Jim," Bony said, when they stood on the ground, "I'd be nervous of camping in that old hut. I'd look around and see these trees, and choose this place to escape the wind and dust. Wouldn't you?"

"Yes, I think I would. It's only just over half a mile to the Bore and water."

"Any horses running in this paddock, say over the last twelve months?"

"Probably the two Nuggety Jack used to pull his car."

"Could be. Still, I rather think the aborigines wouldn't be as particular as you or I when choosing a campsite. Some of those trees have been lopped. Let us prospect."

They found first the mound of ashes indicative of a camp-fire of long duration. They found horse droppings at trees, indicating that the animals had stood for long periods tethered to those trees. Then they found deep depressions, proving that a heavy truck had stood just there for a long period. Under a small mass of brushwood was found a heap of food tins.

"The truck man camped here for more than one night," Pointer said, looking at Bony beneath brows knit. "What in hell for?"

"Today I am feeling like a Civil Servant, Jim. One of those extraordinary persons who never makes a plain statement, who always uses such terms as 'It would appear', 'It might be assumed', 'It could be alleged'.

"It would seem that the truck driver parked his truck here, where he met Nuggety Jack and the horses employed instead of petrol. On the truck were petrol and oil. The aborigine's car was serviced and driven away by the truck driver. When the truck driver returned from whatever mission he was engaged on, he drove off in his truck to the place from which it might be assumed he started. From all the evidence, it could be assumed that a high degree of secrecy was maintained through-out what might be termed unlawful activities. Can you find a plain statement in that lot?"

"Yes. On the truck was petrol and oil."

"Precisely. I could not evade that statement of fact. We will have lunch here and exercise our brains, for now we have to follow the car instead of the truck."

"I would never make a detective, even in my own country," admitted Pointer, and was solaced by:

"How ridiculous would the great FBI and Scotland Yard appear in action in your country, Jim. Let us be serious. The point of major importance in our investigation to date is the secret camp. It was chosen because no one came here, and no stock had been turned into this paddock for several years. The secret camp wasn't the truck man's objective; it was used merely for the change-over from truck to car. But we don't yet know his objective. In what condition does Nuggety Jack keep his car tyres?"

"Pretty good. Actually, Nuggety is a good mechanic."

"Often the case. Well, Jim, I do know that the truck driver carried eighty gallons of additional petrol, and from that we might presume his objective to be some distance from this place. We shall have to do some real sleuthing to pick up his trail, and will succeed only by trial and error. The good general wins by projecting his mind into that of his opposite number. I should do just that . . . project my mind into that of the truck driver. We shall take the track to Blazer's Dam, where you found the body of Brandt."

With Bony once again standing at the back of the driving cabin, Pointer drove past Bore Number Eleven and followed the rarely used bush track to the gate giving entry to the Blazer's Dam paddock. A mile on from this gate, the sandy ground gave place to a gibber field, an extensive area completely covered by gibbers.

These stones, in size a little less than that of a man's palm, are roundish and flattish on the upper surface, and had been polished by wind-driven sand to the smoothness of glass. Here they lay packed together like a man-made garden path put down centuries ago. Where the occasional buckboard and motor vehicle had crossed the field to and from Bore Eleven, the stones had been moved by the wheels, to leave twin ribbons of bare earth.

Pointer was keeping the wheels of the utility to the twin tracks, by habit, and not to avoid the gibbers, when Bony at the back signalled a halt.

"Reverse, and stop instantly when I stamp," shouted Bony. Then: "A little farther. Now go on a foot, not more. Right! Come up and join me."

The overseer complied and Bony waved to the field, where the sun laid a road giving brilliant reflection.

"Where the gibbers reflect the sunlight," Bony said, "see anything?"

Pointer contracted the lids of his eyes, gazed long before shaking his head, admitting he could detect nothing significant.

"No matter. I can see car tracks, Jim. The car turned off and crossed that area of the gibbers. The driver drove as slowly as his engine would permit, in order not to displace the gibbers. But, despite his care, the weight of the car did fractionally disturb every gibber the wheels pressed on, altering the plane of each stone from that it had occupied for many years. The difference is revealed by the sun's light, and could not be humanly observable minus the reflection of the sun. Luck! A few minutes earlier or later, and I wouldn't have seen it."

"Still can't see the tracks," Pointer complained. "But wait a sec. Yes, I think I can now. No, I can't be sure. Damn it! I'm imagining it. Luck, you said. Doesn't eyesight count for anything?"

"Neither eyesight, nor plain reasoning, nor merely common-sense is ever credited to the successful, Jim. It is always luck, they say. Right now in this particular instance, luck or fortune plays a small part. We happen to be here at this vital time, and not an hour before or an hour later. You say you did not see the majesty in the storm which passed over L'Albert before it arrived at Lake Jane. Understandable. We at Lake Jane were favoured by being at a particular angle with the storm-face, and it with the moon. At this moment we are favoured by being at a particular angle with the floor of gibbers with its angle to the line of the sun. If the car continued in that direction, it might ultimately come to the boundary with Lake Jane. Right?"

"That's so. The boundary would be just under twelve miles."

"A gate thereabouts?"

"No. The nearest gate is that on the road from our home-stead to the Lake."

"I remember that one. Let's go. I'll ride with you."

An hour later they became bogged at a creek crossing which looked to be as hard as bitumen. It occupied two laborious hours to get the utility to the far side, and Bony refused to go on until he had had a pannikin of tea, perhaps four.

"Millions of civil servants have afternoon tea, and never miss," he asserted. "I am a civil servant."

The overseer shouted with laughter. Both were smeared with grey mud, and thick slabs of it adhered to boots and legs. Less like a civil servant no human being could ever be.

"Should have brought the private secretary," chortled Pointer. "Or is it the junior typist who makes the afternoon tea for the masters of the taxpayers? Anyway, although you don't look it, I must say you're civil enough, and know your way out of a bog."

From this point the land changed from open sandy spaces to grey soil on which grew box and gum, many of them at mature age when Captain Cook landed at Botany Bay. At this time the prolific growth of herbage concealed the wet patches and water-soaked traps, and Pointer was forced to drive with exceeding care.

As though planned, they arrived at the edge of a wide depression about an hour before nightfall. The hot north wind had blown all day and continued, and the noise of their approach to this large sheet of water was withheld from the waterbirds feeding on it. Pointer stopped the utility on a dry shelf at the very edge, and they looked first at the countless duck and then at each other.

"We have two shotguns," Bony murmured.

"And plenty of cartridges," added Pointer.

"And wood to burn for ashes to cook ducks in."

"And a gnawing hunger for fresh meat."

"That fence crossing the water is the boundary with Lake Jane?"

"That's it, Bony."

"Then we shall camp here, make a cooking fire, shoot duck, and defer our worries until the morning. Guns! Pockets full of cartridges! You go one way. I'll go the other. We'll give each other fifteen minutes to find suitable cover. To hell with detecting and the Civil Service."

Ducks! There were Queensland grey ducks; mountain ducks; black ducks; teal ducks and small divers; pelicans and swans, and cranes and ibis and herons. Far out on the water were even seagulls . . . six hundred miles from the sea. About the edge of the water thousands upon thousands of waterhens ran on their red legs before Bony, and those birds feeding at the water-edge merely swam a little way out, as though to give him passage, and swam to shore after he had passed.

From behind a masking currant bush, Bony waited for Pointer to disturb this aquatic paradise, training his gun on a party of black ducks. When Pointer's gun roared into the wind, Bony fired and, while hastily reloading, counted five ducks bagged by his two barrels.

The picture now became one to remember. The shallow water was beaten to foam by the wings and legs of thousands of birds lifting from it. The air was filled with flashing colours beneath the evening sky, and filled, too, with the sound of wings. Flights and squadrons and fleets of ducks were jet-propelled above him. Now he wasn't the crack shot he had thought to be. When he hit a bird, it was mere chance that his gun was aimed correctly.

Eventually all the ducks departed for another water, and the swans and the pelicans flew at great height, as though to gain a superior bird's-eye view of the uproar. Bony collected eight ducks for about twenty-five cartridges, and was not at all put out when Pointer came back to the utility with seventeen for nineteen cartridges.

"Well, they can't say that we didn't intend to shoot ducks," the overseer claimed. "When do we get home, d'you reckon?"

"Tomorrow, perhaps. Have to get these birds back in good condition. We'd better bag them now, and hang them somewhere to cool for the night." Bony smiled, the sportsman still thrilled, his right shoulder feeling the shock of the gun butt. "Get a good fire going, Jim. I'll take a little walk."

When he came back, Pointer had the camp set up, and a roaring fire making a beacon of light in the deepening dusk. The birds were returning, the big birds followed at intervals by ducks.

"We'll have baked duck for breakfast," Bony said, looking with approval at the fire which would provide the necessary ashes. "I found the place where the car passed through the fence. The driver had, of course, to cut it, but he repaired it before going on. What kind of wire-strainer does Nuggety Jack use?"

"Forked stick he can get out of the scrub," replied Pointer. "Doesn't do too good a job, though."

"Our man used a patent chain wire-strainer he bought at a store. He made a good job of repairing. My! I'm hungry. What's for dinner? Oh, tinned meat again! Wish it was break-fast time."

Pointer agreed, and after they had washed the utensils they sat on their heels well back from the great fire they were burning for the ashes.

"You will remember that girl at Nuggety Jack's camp at Number Ten Bore," Bony said casually, "the one you told that Mrs Long wanted to help out in the house?"

"Yes. Jack's daughter, Lottee. Fine-looking type."

"That's the one. I saw her again yesterday. No marriage mark on her. A virgin, by abo standards, and yet she had a small child clinging to her neck when we saw her at Number Ten."

"The little feller wasn't hers," Pointer said. "That was Missus Dusty's kid."

"There is the point of interest that she wasn't branded in promise of marriage when she was much younger, even when a child. All the others are; all the others I've seen, anyway."

"Lottee is outstanding in many ways," Pointer continued. "Very intelligent. She learnt to speak well, and she can write. Bosses her father and mother. She calls: they run to her. It was said, you know, that Tonto got his beating up for chasing her."

"Twenty-four, Robin told me."

"That would be her age, Bony. Time she was married, isn't it? Fellers are a bit slower than they used to be in my time."

"Could be that they are a little more cautious," argued Bony, and the overseer said:

"Funny you should say that. Lottee has that 'come hither' look, but gives you the 'go to hell' look."

There followed a meditative period, ended by Bony saying:

"Were you a young man, Jim, would you try to hang your hat in her hall?"

Pointer's prompt reply hinted thought along this line. He said:

"Yes, I'd try. But I'd make sure that the door was kept open so I could get out like a bolting rabbit."

CHAPTER 23

The House that Was

JIM POINTER awoke when the dawn was heralding a day of sweet coolness in promise of the autumn. He could hear the birds all about the camp telling of the wrath of the Rain God, roused by the magic rainstones, upon that musty, withering, blasting Thing men called Drought. He saw Bony in the red glow of the fire, still in pyjamas, using the long-handled shovel to dig among the great pile of ash, and bring out several large lumps of baked clay. Sitting sideways on his stretcher, to slip his feet into boots, he heard Bony call:

"Come on, Jim. The tea's made for the first smoke, and breakfast is ready."

"You must have been up early," Pointer said when joining his sporting companion without bothering to dress.

"Couple of hours, Jim. I woke feeling meat-hungry after all the tinned stuff we lived on, and I cooked four succulent ducks for breakfast. Two Queenslanders and two Black ones."

Tea was poured into pannikins, and sugar added, and in the growing light the one smoked his pipe, and the other a cigarette. It would be a good day: a day begun otherwise was doomed to failure.

"We go on, I suppose, trying to trace the car?" Pointer asked, mutely consigning the car to the Devil, for this was paradise for any man.

"Not now, Jim. No talking shop yet. Let us cling to all this until the last second; the caressing warmth of a campfire; the pearly gleam of that sky; the rebirth of Life. Be careful not to step back without looking, because you might step on a teal duck feeding at the edge of the water."

"Certainly gets you in, doesn't it?" Pointer said, sensing rather than detecting the forced cheerfulness in Bony's voice. "I don't wonder that the abos would rather starve than go and live in a government settlement and fatten on plenty."

Bony took him up. "Although they have lived in Australia, they have never possessed it; Australia has ever possessed them. All my life I have had to offer stern resistance, and my father was white. There are times when I sweat, fighting against the siren voice of this land we call Australia."

"I can easily believe it, Bony. I know I would never be happy once I left it to live in a city."

"The Spirit of this Land has you in its grip, all right."

"It has." Pointer flexed his arm muscles and breathed in deeply. "Not only me. It's got Eve as well. I've been on reduced salary for twelve months, and was offered twice the salary to work in a wool store down in Melbourne until the drought broke. Like the blacks, we'd sooner starve."

"I'm reminded of an assignment I was given," Bony said, rolling his second cigarette, if one had sufficient imagination to name it a cigarette. "I was put to locating a feller from Austria. Had inherited a title and family estates, was a brilliant

136

scholar, and quite wealthy in his own right. I had been on the assignment for a month, because the feller was a VIP, and one day I walked over a sandhill and beheld a scene worth painting. Down on the flat was a long and deep waterhole. Near the water was a rough hut. An aboriginal woman was cooking at a fire. Nearby a man sat on a box cleaning a gun, and he was as dark as the woman. Watching him were two children, one about three, the other about two. He was saying something which caused the children to laugh and the woman at the fire to turn her face to them and laugh with them. When I'd told the man my business, and presented certain documents, the man said: 'You think damn fool, eh? You tell them in Austria that I'm going to be a damn fool till the day I die!' "

"I've known white stockmen married to blacks. They seemed happy enough," Pointer said thoughtfully. "Never any rows, arguments, fights."

"Quite so, Jim. They were married to a Something which the woman merely represented. Now let us be married to those ducks."

Stepping from their pyjamas, they walked into the water, Pointer wide of hips and thick of belly, Bony narrow of waist and with a stomach as flat as a board. Having dried and dressed, Bony proceeded to open the clay lumps. He tapped a line down one with the blade of the axe, then broke it open like the halves of an orange. The aroma which rose from that steaming interior! The clay covering had pulled away the feathers of the bird, and the skin, and, cupped like the flesh of the coconut, was breakfast.

"It's worth coming here just for this," sighed Pointer, as he lifted the meat with a fork, so tender was it.

"Another bird to tackle if you like, Jim."

"I'm going to be a stug. Look, if they could cook 'em like this in New York or London, they'd cash in on millions a year."

"And learn something from those awful Orstralians," added Bony.

"Frightful cree-churs," mimicked the overseer. "I'm having another bird if I bust."

"Be careful, Jim. You have to drive."

Thirty minutes later, Pointer was driving the utility to the boundary-fence. There Bony indicated the place which had been cut and repaired, and asked for the overseer's opinion of the work.

The big man studied the method of joining the cut wires, and rubbed his fingers gently along each wire back from the join.

"Chain wire-strainer was used, as you said, Bony. Joins expertly done. More efficiently than Nuggety Jack could ever do." He stared into Bony's watchful eyes. "You find a tree cut down, and the scarf will prove which man did it. You can see a fence, and tell which man built it. The same with this repair job. I know the man who drove the car and repaired this fence."

"Then don't name him, Jim. We must cut it to go through, and repair the cut the best way we can."

"The repairs can wait. There's no stock."

When they had passed through, Bony said:

"On the far side will be the Rudder's Well paddock. Drive direct to the fence, and we'll follow it down to the road gate at Rudder's Well. Might see the tracks of the car."

Pointer was silent and tense all the way to the next fence, where Bony said he would stand at the back to see better. They had now crossed the grey clay country of the ancient river-course, down which water had recently flowed to fill Lake Jane, and were again on the drier red sand and open country.

"We may find tracks along this fence," Bony said quietly. "Don't colour the facts we have with the paint of your imagination. The business of the car driver may have nothing to do with murder."

"He was heading for Rudder's Well," Pointer said stonily. "Four miles from Rudder's Well a man is found dead in a machinery shed. Three miles in the opposite direction his swag was burned with another dead man's bike. You said you weren't liking this. I'm not liking it, either."

Standing at the back of the driver's cabin, Bony could see miles ahead, along the fence, the top of the mill at Rudder's Well. Ceaselessly he watched the passing ground, patiently hoping for further signs of the car which had come into this paddock seven months before.

As they neared the gate where he had waylaid and branded Tonto, the scrub changed from bull oak and mulga to box and canegrass growing on claypan soil. The canegrass recalled to mind the open shed at Rudder's Well, and from that to the picture of the secret bower amid the tea tree. That would be away to his right, say two miles.

138

Then he saw that which made him stamp a foot to stop the utility.

"Angle to the west," he shouted to Pointer. "Nose into the scrub at the end of the canegrass."

At the extremity of the canegrass, the branches of a box tree were blackened as by fire, and the new leaf growth was thick on the branches having now no finer twigs. Pointer stopped close to this tree, and through the windscreen he stared at a large patch of fire-stained ground. Behind him, Bony looked down on the square of blackened earth, on which lay twisted wire-netting and knots of plain wire.

Pointer backed from the seat and Bony jumped down from the back, and both stood without speaking while reading this page of the Book of the Bush.

"Peculiar place to build a canegrass hut or shed," Pointer said, grimly. "Nearest water over half a mile away. What the hell would the Downers build a shed here for?"

Bony took the shovel and scraped the earth away at one corner of the burned area. He uncovered the unburned end of a corner post. He stepped along two sides and assessed the area of the building that had been. It was fourteen feet by ten. The position of the knotted wires showed where the cross beams had been, to carry the thatched roof.

"The place was burned down months before the rain," he said. "No deep ash sludge, because the wind had blown off the ashes."

Bony left, walking towards the fence and the distant mill and well beyond it. Pointer took the shovel and began poking about with the tip of its blade. Presently Bony returned to say that no one at Rudder's Well, or on the road, could possibly see the building as it had been.

"Doesn't look as though anyone lived here for even a night," Pointer said. "There's no refuse, no food tins, nothing."

"Could have been buried or carted away," Bony countered.

He went to the burned tree, studied its branches, faced to the south. The ground was sandy above a harder surface. He walked out from the tree, scraped the sand with the heel of his boot. Pointer joined him with the shovel.

"What are you looking for?" he asked.

"Oil. Give me the shovel."

With the shovel Bony scraped the sand from the under-surface. The oil was there. Under the windblown sand covering was the oil mark, proving where the car had stood. Pointer said:

"Place must have been burned down on purpose, Bony. Anyway, there's no bones among the wire. But why? Why build a shed or hut here? Doesn't make any sort of sense. You any ideas?"

"Yes." Bony's face was expressionless, and the overseer waited. "Not now, Jim. I want proof. Nearly midday. Let's boil the billy and have lunch."

They spoke rarely during the meal, both standing and pensively gazing at the site of the fire, and trying to re-create the scene prior to the burning. After the meal Bony smoked three cigarettes before beginning the customary circling of the place, each circle wider than the one previously completed.

He found where the canegrass had been chopped from the clumps. Found no marks of a truck or car, and the grass must have been bundled and carried to the building site.

On rejoining the overseer, he said:

"I have stood on this place and have circled it. I have communed with it, trying to reverse the progress of Time, to go back to when there stood a house, and what happened in it. Are you sensitive to things and places? I am, often. I feel no evil in this place; in this place which was, now is not, and never will be again. All right, Jim. We'll get on back. Nothing here for us. Circle wide of Lake Jane. We won't call on the Downers today."

They had been driving for an hour without a word spoken by either of them when Pointer stopped the utility and turned on the seat to look at Bony.

"When we get home, what do we say, or do? There's Robin, remember."

"We say we had good shooting, and we present the ducks as proof." Bony rolled and lit a cigarette, then turned slightly to confront the overseer with blue, steady gaze. "Jim, listen. You know a little and guess a lot. I know a lot and guess a little. I told you I was looking into a fog. I still am. I cannot say to anyone: 'You did this or that against the Law.' Not yet. Therefore, we enjoyed our shooting trip, and we hope everyone at L'Albert will enjoy the ducks."

Pointer drove on.

"A crime is often like the impact of a stone on water," eventually Bony said. "From it spread ripples to affect in various ways innocent persons, and persons not so innocent. Because you know a little and guess a great deal, I believe you are jumping to conclusions. That is most unwise. Your girl may suffer hurt, or she may not. Be easy, Jim."

It was not till after five o'clock that they reached L'Albert, and while the overseer was telling about the shooting and displaying the bag, Bony sauntered to the office and spoke to Sergeant Mawby.

CHAPTER 24

The Inquisition

ALTHOUGH Sergeant Mawby and Constable Sefton left Mindee one hour after Bony called them, they did not arrive until the next morning at seven-thirty. Midnight Long piloted them from the river homestead, otherwise they might have been delayed still more. A few hours' sleep at Fort Deakin had helped on this tiresome journey.

After breakfast the police party occupied the common room at the men's quarters, and held a short conference.

"I am gratified by your swift and willing co-operation, Sergeant Mawby," Bony said at the opening. "That also applies to you, Constable Sefton. I shall remember it in my Final Report."

"Thank you, sir. It's been a pleasure to work with you," responded Mawby, and Sefton nodded agreement.

"Good! Now we'll get to current business," Bony continued. "You have gained information of a vital nature, which enabled me to crack this case of the two murders, for the murder of Dickson must be associated with the murder of Brandt. I use the verb 'crack' advisedly because I have yet to break open the case. It has been exceptionally involved, as you will learn, and it has presented difficulties in time and terrain which, you will agree, were not easy to conquer.

"I am still uncertain of the motive for the two murders; and I'm still not crystal-clear on many points. Therefore, our proceedings must be in the form of an inquiry from which we may be justified in taking action. As we have to examine several aborigines, we will adopt the slightly unusual course of making a show of the inquiry. You agree, Sergeant? This is your State, not mine."

Mawby squared his wide shoulders, expelled his breath, and said:

"You're the boss, sir. Carry on."

"Then, Sefton, please inform Mr Long and Mr Pointer that we would like them to be with us. Immediately you have done so, round up all the aborigines and park them outside till required."

"Yes, sir." Sefton's dark eyes were amused, and Bony's liking for him increased.

Bony returned to Mawby.

"I refrained from going over you to the Superintendent in Broken Hill, because I wanted to keep this affair in the family as it were." The left eyelid drooped. "Mrs Mawby would doubtless find the change to the coast mountains beneficial for her sinus trouble, don't you think?"

Mawby sighed. "Now if you could wangle that, Inspector . . ."

"One never knows what waits beyond the bend. Ah! Mr Long and Mr Pointer. I was hoping you would consent to be present. Perhaps even consent to assist us, unofficially, of course. Now, I sit here, with Sergeant Mawby to take notes for me, and the victims will be seated opposite to me. Please be seated by the wall there and refrain from comment. We are to deal with members of a most ancient race. This isn't a court, as you, Mr Long, being a Justice of the Peace, will know. Yes, Constable?"

"The aborigines are outside, sir. All but the young woman Lottee Jack. Miss Pointer informed me that she saw Lottee Jack running into the bush."

"That is certainly a matter of interest," Bony said aside to Mawby. "All right, Constable, bring the aborigine named Dusty, and then stand by at the door to see that none of the other aborigines clears away into the bush."

Dusty appeared, urged forward politely by Sefton, and was greeted with a beaming smile from Bony. He was invited to sit at the table, and this he did with a lithe grace and no sign of nervousness.

"Now, Dusty, the Aborigines Department, which you know gives you people protection, has asked us to find out why you bashed up poor Tonto. I have to write a letter to them about this. I don't want to make it bad for you with the Aborigines Department, so we'll have to go slow, won't we? I have been told that you and the bucks gave Tonto a hell of a hiding for lying down sick instead of going to Lake Jane and letting the dogs off their chains after Paul Dickson was killed. The other night I went out to Number Ten to ask Tonto if this was true, and he wasn't there. Would you know where he is?"

"No fear, Inspector," replied Dusty without hesitation. "I told Tonto to stay there until we got back from getting the rain-making wages." Dusty laughed loudly. "You see, Inspector, Tonto was out trapping a fox the other night and he ran himself into a wire fence. Got a lot of cuts on his face. Didn't want Mr Pointer to see him like that."

"Well, Dusty, the Aborigines Department is going crook about Tonto being bashed up. You know that the Department could have you all taken down to the Settlement. You can't go bashing up a young buck just because he was sick and he didn't let the Lake Jane dogs off."

Dusty was now not quite so perky. He fidgeted in his chair, glanced at Sergeant Mawby, who was looking at the ceiling, then turned to look at Sefton, and finally turned to take stock of Long and the overseer. When again facing Bony he said:

"Tonto's lazy feller. Cheeky, too."

"You know how it is, Dusty," Bony proceeded after cogitating. "You're the Medicine Man. You say for Tonto to unchain Lake Jane dogs, then Tonto must unchain 'em. That's Blackfeller Law, isn't it?"

"Too right, boss." Over Dusty's lean face slowly spread a grin which had little of humour in it. He broke into low laughter. "You cunnin' feller, all right, Inspector. Too bloody true."

"I'm only trying to get you fellers off the hook, Dusty. Now you go outside and rub your churinga stones against your forehead, and think up a yarn I can send down to the Aborigines Department." Bony turned to Sefton: "Ask Nuggety Jack to step in for a moment."

Sefton knew his job, and he was outside before Dusty could say two words to the head man. Bony took the sergeant and both manager and overseer into his questioning gaze.

"Tell me, please. Was Tonto thrashed because he failed to obey the order to free the Lake Jane dogs after Dickson was murdered, and before the Downers arrived home from Mindee?"

"Although Dusty didn't admit so in words, it's obvious," replied Long, and Mawby smiled, saying: "You cunnin' feller, all right, Inspector. Too bloody true."

"So we begin," Bony said briskly. "Oh! Come in, Nuggety Jack. Sit down . . . there. Make yourself easy. Want to ask you something."

The head man, of cubic proportions, caused the chair to creak. He smiled widely, first at Bony, then at Mawby, and Mawby winked, and Nuggety did likewise. Abruptly, Bony frowned.

"What's all that noise out there?" he demanded of Sefton. Nuggety Jack replied, laughing again.

"Only my missus yowling, Inspector. She thinks you're gonna chop off me head."

"Chop off your head? Why?" exclaimed the astonished inspector.

"Well, you know what women are," responded Nuggety, loudly laughing, and winked again at Mawby. "Different to what it usta be. In the old days a feller belted his wife every morning and was the boss. Now the Department says you mustn't do that. And the women they say, 'You never do no work. I washes me fingers to the bone for Missus Pointer and you all grab the bacco.' Women!"

"Ah, yes, women!" smiled Bony. "Always on a feller's back. Still, it wasn't women I wanted you to tell me about. I'd like to know if you have seen any strange feller about the run lately."

The smile remained, but the black eyes became crafty.

"Only stranger feller's been that white bloke killed over at Lake Jane. You know, that Dickson feller."

"I know about him." Bony frowned. "What about the Jorkin boys at the Soak? Ever see them?"

Nuggety Jack was a different proposition from Dusty. He shook his head, continued to smile, but lowered shutters behind his black eyes.

"If it wasn't one of the Jorkins, who was it who camped with you out at Number Eleven – you know, the camp in the black oak?"

"Oh, that feller!" Memory flooded into Nuggety's face. "That was long time back. 'Bout this time last year. That was Ed Jorkin. He was out kangarooing. I remember him."

Mawby didn't fail to observe the shutters behind the black

eyes, and wondered what the heck Bony was leading to. Of the others, only Pointer saw the trap being prepared for Nuggety. The woman outside continued to wail, and sympathizers were wailing with her. Bony wrote a note importantly, and passed it to the sergeant. The sergeant read and whistled astonishment. He passed the note to Sefton, and Nuggety returned his attention to Bony, the smile vanquished, the unknown growing to become terror. Bony brought the tips of his fingers together and looked sternly over them at the head man.

"You could be on your way to jail for a long time, Nuggety Jack. You one big liar, eh! Those Jorkin boys run around in old bombs. That feller who camped with you that time out at Number Eleven was driving a truck!"

"A truck!" exploded Nuggety Jack. "Why didn't you say that before? That feller didn't do no camping. He took out a dozen bags of chaff for the horses, 'cos Mr Pointer wouldn't sell me no petrol 'cos the store stock was low. Eh, Mr Pointer? That's right. You remember?"

The overseer remained silent. Bony said clearly and calmly, as a judge on his bench:

"Who was the truck driver?"

"Stranger to me, Inspector. Come from Broken Hill. Just brought that chaff, that's all. Unloaded it, had a drink of tea, then went off back."

"What was his name?"

"What the hell!" shouted Nuggety, and stood. "Look you . . ."

"Constable, arrest that man."

Sefton was swift. Nuggety Jack couldn't see them, but he could feel the irons imprisoning his wrists behind his back.

"Take him out and anchor him to something solid in the machinery shed, Constable," ordered Bony. "Then bring in his wife. Must stop that screeching."

The wailing became universal when the prisoner emerged into the sunlight. Mawby had become anxious but still retained confidence in Bony. Bony stood and crossed to Pointer.

"Jim, we must be easy with this woman. She will not be fearful of you, and you can treat her gently. You have followed the trend of my questioning. You are *au fait* with the outline of our recent trip. You know who drove that truck. I am asking you to take my place to disclose the whys and the wherefores."

Pointer was greatly troubled. He said:

"Don't you know the whys and the wherefores?"

"Yes, but I must have confirmation."

"Very well."

Bony sat against the wall with Midnight Long, Mawby expelled caught breath. The Fort Deakin manager stared at the floor between his feet.

Mrs Jack, small and usually so energetic and bossy, was brought in and seated by Sefton. The row outside continued. The woman was sobbing loudly, and Pointer leaned across the table and patted her comfortingly.

"It's all right, Florrie. Now be quiet for a while. If Nuggety Jack's in trouble, then we must try to get him out of it. Nuggety won't answer our questions about what happened out at Eleven Bore that time you were camped there and a feller came on a truck and borrowed his car. You just tell me all about that. Go on, now. There's nothing much to cry about."

The lubra gazed pleadingly at Pointer, the tears streaming down her withering face, and in that moment the overseer hated the policemen, Nuggety Jack, and himself.

CHAPTER 25

Slaves of the Bush

IT WAS eleven o'clock, and on his veranda John Downer stood to welcome the travellers in the car which stopped at the steps.

"Good day!" he shouted. "Come on up. The kettle's boiling."

Sergeant Mawby alighted and Bony appeared. They mounted the steps together and John gave them warm welcome, and appeared not to be perturbed by their unsmiling faces.

"Come on in," he cried. "Eric's getting morning lunch. Great day, eh! All green and fresh, and don't the grass grow?"

They followed him into the kitchen, to see Eric standing with his back to the stove.

"May as well all sit down," Mawby said heavily. "Inspector Bonaparte has something to deal with."

He was watching Eric, legs like springs coiled ready for

triggering, and he manoeuvred to sit at the table side with him. It was pathetic how the joyousness faded from John's face, to be replaced by perplexity.

A complete silence fell, as three men watched one rolling several cigarettes to place in a little pile. The blue eyes regarded John for a long moment, and then examined Eric, who had slowly made but one cigarette.

"I'll talk to you, Eric, because I believe you can assist me in my investigation of the deaths of Paul Dickson and Carl Brandt," Bony said. "That happened a long time ago, but the print in the Book of the Bush doesn't quickly vanish.

"On September 8th, last year, you and your father reached Mindee, at the start of your annual holiday. On September 18th you left Mindee, ostensibly to travel to Broken Hill, where you have friends, leaving your father in Mindee. That morning you left Mindee you purchased two 40-gallon drums of petrol, an 8-gallon case of engine oil, a chain wire-strainer, and certain foodstuffs and clothing. Ten miles along the road to Broken Hill, you branched off on a track taking you to the Northern Road, and you proceeded then as far as a point two miles from Jorkin's Soak, where you left the road and drove across country to Bore Eleven. Would you care to tell me why you did that?"

"What the hell are you driving at, Bony?" shouted the old man.

"Quiet, Dad. Leave this to me," Eric said, and turned to Bony. "I could not discuss my private affairs under these circumstances."

"Then I will continue, Eric. After crossing Walton's Creek you drove to the gate into Bore Number Eleven Paddock. You parked the truck among a clump of black oak, where Nuggety Jack was waiting with his car, which had been hauled there by his horses. With him was his wife, his daughter Lottee, Dusty the Medicine Man, and Dusty's wife.

"You serviced Nuggety Jack's car, and you loaded it with spare petrol and food, for a trip of some days. With Lottee Jack as your passenger, you drove the car to the Blazer's Dam Paddock, through the gate for a mile, and turned off on a field of gibbers. On coming to the boundary fence, you cut that, and repaired it with the chain wire-strainer. Then you crossed the Lake Jane homestead paddock to a canegrass shed or hut which is within half a mile of Rudder's Well, but cannot be seen from the Well or the road to it. Am I right?"

"Go on, lad. Tell him he's making it all up," urged John, and when Eric remained stonily silent: "Damn it, is it true?"

"It's true enough, John," Bony said.

"So what if it is?" shouted the old man. "What's wrong in running off with a black wench? Fine-looking lass. Caught my eye more'n once. Made me wish I was young again. Nothing in seducing an abo wench. Crikey! Plenty of that done down through the years. Wenches like that'll lie down for a plug of chewing-tobacco."

"Stop it!" shouted Eric, now on his feet, his fist raised to his father. "Shut up! You keep your dirty mind out of this."

"All right, lad. All right. No need to blow your top."

With his left hand Mawby pulled Eric down to his chair, keeping his right hand beneath the table edge. John was seething with anger, not wholly directed to Bony.

"After a period spent at that canegrass hut," Bony went on, you and Lottee Jack returned to the camp in the black oaks, and from there you drove back to Mindee. You arrived in Mindee on October 5th, and on the 10th you came home with your father. It is presumed that Brandt and Dickson were murdered on or about October 1st."

Bony waited for Eric to speak, and old Downer sat silent and constantly clenching and unclenching his hands.

"On the first of October, Eric, you and Lottee were living at that canegrass hut which is within half a mile of Rudder's Well and less than four miles from this homestead, where the body of Paul Dickson was discovered by you and your father. And this is not country on which live thousands of people per square mile.

"In the late afternoon of the 12th, Sergeant Mawby and Constable Sefton, with Mr Long and two aborigines, plus a tracker, returned to L'Albert, the aborigines sent up a smoke signal to Nuggety Jack and those with him, telling Lottee that she had to meet you as soon as possible. I am reasonably sure that on leaving the grass hut you burned it down, and that Lottee, or both of you, fashioned a love nest among the tea tree one mile this side of the hut. There you met Lottee and cut her hair, and the hair you burned between two sandalwood trees, and buried the ashes as an aborigine would have done.

"You were married to Lottee blackfeller-style, and at that ceremony a lock of her hair was cut and presented to you as Lottee's man. She was wearing that lock of hair as a charm when Dickson was murdered, and he clutched it in his hand

148

when he died. It wasn't noticed until you returned from Mindee, when both your father and you saw it.

"You foresaw that that lock of hair would be a vital clue if
you didn't do something about it to confuse the issue, because
scientific examination would prove from whose head it came.
It was brilliant of you to take from your mother's Treasure
Chest those two locks of hair, the one preserved from your own
head and the other from your father's. To make that appear
as robbery you also removed the watch, and disordered the
kitchen to make it appear there had been a struggle between
Dickson and Brandt.

"Had you stopped at that point all might have been well
with you, for you did slew the police off the trail. The hair cut
from Lottee's head was long, and so you cut her hair short
just in case the police did associate her with the hair in
Dickson's hand. Your really great mistake was when you
brushed out the tracks about the love nest in the tea tree, for
then you carried the trea tree branch to the sandalwoods, where
there was no tea tree, and left it there after brushing out your
tracks and burying the fire ash.

"Sergeant Mawby will be taking you into custody on suspicion for the murder of Dickson and Brandt. When you were
living with Lottee at the grass hut, you were discovered by
one of those two men.

"He was killed to preserve the secret of your marriage to
Lottee under Blackfeller Law. To your consternation, the
other man appeared when you had a body on your hands, and
he was killed. You burned their swags and Brandt's bike in a
gilgie hole. You arranged Dickson's body in your machinery
shed, and you took the body of Brandt eighteen miles to bury
it in a sandhill. Thus you staged the murder of Dickson by
Brandt. Unfortunately for you, a wind storm blew the sand off
the body, which was found by Pointer. But you had something
like six weeks' start before the police were brought back from
chasing after a dead man, and you were confident that no
investigation would succeed in bringing the facts to light. You
had never heard of me."

Bony stopped speaking, and lit one of his cigarettes.

Seriously, Eric said: "You are certainly one out of the box.
But tell me: why should I have killed those two men when
Lottee and I were married, even in blackfeller fashion?"

"Because your early environment was too strong to permit

149

you to acknowledge a liaison with an aborigine woman. You have many strengths and many weaknesses; one weakness being the dread of what is commonly called 'loss of face', in your case, what will your old school friends say of you; what will Robin Pointer and her parents say; what will all the people of Mindee and your friends in Broken Hill say, when they hear you are living with an aborigine?"

"You are less than half right, Bony," Eric said earnestly.

"I know that."

"You do?"

"Of course. My mother having been an aborigine."

Sitting with his elbows on the table, and his chin resting on his entwined fingers, Eric Downer regarded Bony with peculiar intensity, and Bony regarded him with slight uneasiness. Throughout this interview Eric had not reacted as all those others had done when listening to the case built against them. He betrayed no sign of fear. On the contrary he was now as a man from whom a load of responsibility has been lifted, and for the first time he appeared to Bony without any inhibitions. Even his father was looking at him curiously, almost gladly, as though realizing his son had recovered from a dangerous illness.

"You made remarkably few mistakes," Bony went on. "None of them were silly, because no full white man would have recognized them. For instance, had you been frank with Robin, had you told her of your love for Lottee and your subjection to a power which emanated through Lottee, I am sure Robin would not have painted 'Never the Twain shall Meet', and would not have betrayed in many little things her suspicion, amounting to certainty, that you were in close association with Lottee. She was hoping that your infatuation would pass, when you would return to her.

"No full white man would have suspected that the bashing of Tonto was connected in any way with the death of your dogs and the near death of Bluey, following the murder of Dickson. When Tonto admitted his dereliction of duty, you stood forth, because no aborigine would account the matter as worthy of thrashing Tonto nearly to death. It was your righteous anger, roused by the unnecessary cruelty to animals, which betrayed you."

Bony sighed, and Eric continued to look at him without fear, and without perturbation.

"I give you a credit mark, Eric," and Mawby frowned as though he disapproved of giving credit marks to any criminal. "Your spurious attitude towards the aborigines in general might, had it not been for those other slips, especially that of tossing aside the tea tree branch in the wrong place, have delayed my investigation by many months. Your scoffing at the rain-making was in accordance with your environment and school background, but it was spurious in any man so closely associated with the aborigines as you were."

Eric glanced at the clock, then with his chin still resting on his fists he closed his eyes. Bony struck a match, although his cigarette was alight, and Eric's eyes remained closed for another forty seconds. On again looking at Bony, he smiled and nodded his head at something giving him satisfaction. The others remained still, silent and watchful.

"Shall I tell you why you acted as you did in this affair with Lottee?" asked Bony, and Eric shrugged. "Where another white man could take a black woman with a laugh of indifference at public opinion, you could not face public opinion. Another white man deeply loving a black woman could marry her openly and to the devil with public opinion. But not you, and, I do believe, not even Lottee. The only concession you made was to go through the aborigines' marriage rite, and keep that secret. Now listen to me finding excuses for you.

"You found yourself in the grip of a power you couldn't resist. You knew it was wrongful to submit, precisely as the alcoholic is aware that for him it is wrong to drink. I know this power. I have had to fight it all my life. I know men who were like you, and men who have been as I am, strong to resist. Robin Pointer has sensed it; we can see that in her paintings. I should be the very last to condemn you for surrendering to this power which we call The Spirit of the Bush. I do condemn you for the weakness you have displayed by paying servile deference to public opinion. You wanted to have your cake, and to eat it.

"That subject, however, lies between you and me, Eric, because there is that which influences both of us. The other matter, the matter of the death of those two men, is a matter of the State, and I am a servant of the State, sworn to uphold its laws. You will be held for murder."

"All right, Bony." Eric smiled again. "You have been astonishingly understanding, but only ninety per cent so.

151

What Lottee and I have is something which even public opinion must not be allowed to shadow. It goes so deep that even you haven't grasped it. It is so high that we can attain it only through death. When I tell you that Lottee and I have slept together for many nights, and that both of us are virgins this day, you can make up that ten per cent deficiency."

"It explains much," admitted Bony. "It makes me regret that I . . . and Sergeant Mawby . . . have to do our duty."

"There is a way open for us, and relief from regret for you," Eric said. "All right, Lottee, take over."

Lottee stood in the doorway to Eric's bedroom, to which she must have gained access through the open window. She was then behind both Eric and Sergeant Mawby. Until she spoke, neither Mawby nor John Downer knew she was there, and Bony now realized how close was she with Eric, and he with her. A few moments before, when Eric sat with closed eyes, she was telling she had come. Doubtless, she had warned him of danger, and had told him she was leaving L'Albert to join him.

She had the men covered with a .32 Winchester repeating rifle. She could see Bony observing her, and he saw that she wasn't menacing him in particular. Eric sat unmoving. Bony said:

"Sergeant Mawby, you will remove your right hand from your revolver, and place it on the table with the left hand . . . until I countermand this order." Amazement was enthroned on Mawby's face. He obeyed, and Lottee said:

"Thank you, Inspector. I don't want to shoot anyone."

Keeping her back to the wall, she slipped to the veranda doorway, where Mawby and old John and Bony could see her, and her rifle. "Eric, please go out the back door and up the veranda steps to come behind me."

"Damnation! What is this, Inspector? You aiding and abetting," growled Mawby, fury heightening his apparent unleashed strength.

"I have not yet completed my assignment, Sergeant. Until I do, I shall not permit you to commit suicide."

"Good advice, Sarge," snapped Downer. "Lottee's the kind that can't miss. Against her principles. Lottee, point that gun somewhere else, to make sure you don't kill anyone."

"I shan't miss, Mr Downer," she said. Eric appeared

behind her, taller than she, and with the light of the zealot blazing in his eyes. Again the girl spoke: "It is time for us to go to another country."

She wore only white shorts. The dilly-bag of crimson silk divided her breasts. She was sweetly beautiful and her eyes glowed like black opal. Bony felt himself being drawn down from his ivory tower of vanity and achievement by this Power against which he had so long fought, and drops of moisture were gathering on his forehead.

The girl's ego dominated them, hedged them about. Even Mawby's anger was subdued by it so that he waited on events with resignation.

"Ever since we were small children, Eric has belonged to me, and I have belonged to him," Lottee said. "It has come from the trees and the sandy places, and all the wild things, this loving which binds us. I have never struggled against it. Eric has, but it was too strong for him.

"All the Inspector said about the secret camp and Eric coming there for me is true. We had the little hidey-house built ready for us. We planned to stay there, sleep together, and be sure that our love was stronger than just mating. Then we were going to be married white-feller-fashion in Mindee church. And we were strong too. I was no black girl to lie down for a plug of tobacco, Mr Downer.

"No, you let me talk now. We had been in our hidey-house for many days and nights, when one morning early I went to the well for water. I passed close to the shed, and then a stranger white-man jumped at me and threw me down and raped me. And then he laughed, and I could have killed a dozen men. I killed him with a tyre lever that was in the shed. When he was dead he was covered with blood, and so was I.

"I ran to the trough and lay down in it, and I pressed the ball valve so that water gushed over me and on along the trough to spill over and take his filthy blood with it. After a while I got out and lay down beside the trough. I think I went unconscious. I must have. I woke up, and there was Brandt looking down at me, and his eyes said what the other man's eyes had said. I stood up and he made a grab for me, and suddenly I knew I still had the tyre lever. And I killed him, too."

The low, vibrant voice stopped, when the ticking clock became noise. Bony waited for the voice to speak again, for it was the mother voice he had never known and always longed to hear.

"We planned to make it look like Brandt killed the stranger and then ran away. We burned our hidey-house and wiped out tracks. We had to leave the dogs tied up because they would have followed us, and Tonto was told to come and let them go.

"When Eric left in his truck to go back to Mindee, I found I'd lost my marriage hair, and then when Eric saw it clutched in the stranger's hand, and he knew his father saw it too, he took the hair from his mother's Treasure Chest, and took the watch to make it look like robbery. I'll be leaving my dilly-bag on the veranda, and you'll find the watch and hair in it.

"That's all, except one thing. Dusty and Nuggety and mother took me into the bush, and I was made good again, black-feller fashion, with fire-heated gibbers. I did not scream. Pain gave me back my virginity.

"Then we planned what we are going to do now, if those murders were ever found out. We can't let you part us. One of us would surely die, and the other would always be only a half. In the Spirit we shall dwell in the trunk of a tree, as all blackfellers do."

"No!" shouted John. "No!"

The lovers vanished and the door slammed shut.

CHAPTER 26

A Tree shall Receive Them

"THEY'LL BE after my car," growled Mawby. "Do I sit like this all day?"

"Patience often has saved a man his life," Bony averred, and lit a cigarette with fingers which trembled. "Those two aren't petty thieves, Mawby. We shall never see their like."

Old John lurched to his feet and made for the veranda door. Bony let him go, knowing he would not be shot. He and Mawby followed him out to the veranda rail.

The lovers were walking down the slope of waving grass, the blue heeler trotting beside Eric. His arm was about Lottee's waist, and Lottee continually looked back over a shoulder, the rifle ready in her hand. Before them the red-legged waterhens rose in fluttering clouds to swirl about them like black confetti.

When the 'escapees' were beyond Mrs Downer's grave, the sergeant made no use of the steps to reach the ground. Eric went on down to the boat, and the girl aimed her rifle at the running man. Sand and grass spurted upwards a yard to Mawby's left, and he went to ground as a chased fox into its hole.

"The gal ain't aiming to kill him, Bony," groaned old John. "But if he makes her she will." He shouted: "Come back here, you fool!"

Another bullet spurted dangerously close when the sergeant made his next rush, ending behind a corner post of the grave-yard. Bony could see Eric's head and shoulders above the low shore dunes. He was standing in the boat and calling to Lottee. Arrowheads of ducks were flashing low above the man and the girl who was running to join him. Fleets of pelicans and swans were now off the water and gaining height. The 'confetti' appeared to be following the lovers, and Sergeant Mawby looked to be running into it.

Now the boat could be seen from the veranda. Eric was standing facing the bow and paddling Indian-fashion, with Lottee crouched at the stern, and training her weapon on the dunes where Mawby would appear. Neither Bony nor John looked at the approaching car racing up from the Crossing. Old John went down the steps, and ran towards the Lake.

On Mawby reaching the shore dunes and gallantly standing upright, the boat was four hundred yards from the shore. Bony could see him firing his revolver into the air, but dimly heard the reports, and the sergeant's voice not at all, such was the birds' commotion.

The car stopped with brakes complaining, and Mawby came running up the slope, passing old John and taking no notice of him. From the car emerged Robin Pointer and Constable Sefton, and they stood looking at the boat beyond the cloud of waterhens. Sefton received Mawby's wrath.

"What the hell you doing here? I left you to keep an eye on the abos. Go on, say it."

Sefton, tall and rangy, bore the explosion by indicating Robin and shrugging, and Robin raced up the steps to Bony. "I had to come. I made Sef. bring me, as father wouldn't let me drive. What are they doing out there? What's it mean?"

Bony neither spoke nor turned to her, standing erect with

his dark hands whitened by the grip on the veranda rail. The boat was a long way out. On the dune John Downer stood with the dog sitting beside him. What he was shouting they could not hear, although momentarily the waterhens were settling, and he was becoming ever more clearly seen.

A thousand yards from the shore, Eric swung the oar about his head and flung it far away. He stooped to Lottee and took the rifle and flung it away too. Again he stooped to do something to the bottom of the boat.

Bony knew that the last strand was severed. He, who stood between two races and sometimes bridged them with his sympathetic heart, exulted in the ideal which this event would enthrone in his memory for ever.

The man and the woman stood in the boat and embraced, their feet spread four-square to maintain balance. The water birds skittered on the water about them, and a fleet of pelicans passed above them, circled and became water borne beyond them.

Those on the veranda could see the boat settling, and in a frenzy Robin clutched Bony's arm, and cried out:

"What are they doing?"

Sefton answered for Bony:

"Better not look, Robin. Eric's pulled out the plug."

The moments passed, and, had there been doubt, now there was none. Again Robin shook Bony's arm, and this time whispered:

"Bony! Look! They'll be drowned. Why? Eric! Why Eric?"

When he turned to her she shrank from the bleakness of his eyes.

"You said something, Robin?"

"I did. What are they going to do?"

"Give the lie to your picture 'Never the Twain shall Meet'."

The boat disappeared, and for a moment the man and the woman appeared to be standing on the water. Robin turned from Bony to Sefton, and the tall policeman slipped an arm about her, and pressed her face into his uniform shirt. Swiftly the lovers sank, still fast in that embrace. The birds were drawing in above them. The man and the dog were motionless on the dune.

Somewhere a tree stood waiting with its branches wide.

Best of American Crime

PATRICIA HIGHSMITH

'A mistress of suspense — a first-class writer' TIME AND TIDE

THIS SWEET SICKNESS 3/6
THE CRY OF THE OWL 3/6
DEEP WATER 3/6
THE TWO FACES OF JANUARY 3/6

JOHN D. MACDONALD

'A first-rate craftsman of crime. Hardly a suspense writer can surpass him'
NEW YORK TIMES

HURRICANE 2/6
DEATH TRAP 2/6
THE CROSSROADS 2/6
THE NEON JUNGLE 3/6
THE DROWNER 3/6
THE PRICE OF MURDER 3/6
DEADLY WELCOME 3/6

HILLARY WAUGH

'Stands alone as a writer of thrillers that are different' MANCHESTER EVENING NEWS

JIGSAW 2/6
LAST SEEN WEARING 2/6
ROAD BLOCK 2/6
THE LATE MRS. D 3/6
BORN VICTIM 3/6
DEATH AND CIRCUMSTANCE 3/6
PRISONER'S PLEA 3/6

CHARLES WILLIAMS

'One of the best of the newer American writers of tough intelligent thrillers'
BOOKS AND BOOKMEN

THE SAILCLOTH SHROUD 2/6
THE LONG SATURDAY NIGHT 2/6
THE CATFISH TANGLE 3/6
DEAD CALM 3/6

Joyce Porter

First two in a new series featuring
Chief Inspector Wilfred Dover, fat, lazy
and dyspeptic, the bane of Scotland Yard
and his long-suffering Sergeant
MacGregor.

DOVER ONE 3/6

The first of the cases more or less
solved by Inspector Dover.
The 16-stone, red-haired femme fatale of
a Creedshire village disappears,
but where could one hide
a body like that — dead or alive?

DOVER TWO 3/6

Once again Sergeant MacGregor does
the work and Inspector Dover gets the
credit as the intrepid pair investigate the
strange case of the girl who was
murdered twice, and startle everyone
by solving the mystery.

'A joy . . . Dover is unquestionably the
most entertaining as well as the most
repellent detective in fiction' GUARDIAN

'Joyce Porter will soon be among
the most widely-read
of women crime writers' EXPRESS & STAR

John Sanders

Two superb historical thrillers introducing **NICHOLAS PYM** — Bond-style agent in Cromwell's Intelligence service.

'Both in the five-star class' DAILY MIRROR

A FIREWORK FOR OLIVER 3/6

Pym's mission is to find and suppress a newly-invented gun—a weapon so revolutionary that its very existence is a threat to the Protectorate and the life of Cromwell himself . . .

'All the thrills of a tough Secret Service thriller coupled to a Roundhead and Cavalier romance' SUNDAY CITIZEN

'Tremendous pace . . . breath-taking adventures' ABERDEEN PRESS AND JOURNAL

THE HAT OF AUTHORITY 3/6

Pym turns sea captain to snatch a fortune in gold on the Spanish Main— pitting his wits against the Royalists and the forces behind the dreaded Spanish inquisition.

'007 would be proud of Mr. Pym's performance' ABERDEEN EVENING PRESS

BRITISH BATTLES SERIES (Illustrated)

The Spanish Armada 5/-

MICHAEL LEWIS

'A distinguished addition to the series.
A brilliantly clear picture of the campaign,
the conditions leading up to it, and the state
of affairs resulting in both countries.'
BRITISH BOOK NEWS

'A clear, concise description, eschewing
the more fanciful David and Goliath
interpretation and concentrating instead
on naval realities, the people involved,
their ships and guns...A fine book.'
YORKSHIRE POST

'The naval expert to whom we chiefly owe
our new knowledge of the event.'
LISTENER

For information about current and
forthcoming PAN titles write to:

PAN LIST
PAN BOOKS LTD 33-TOTHILL STREET
LONDON SW1